ARDYBO
DVENTURES™

PA

HARDYBOYS ADVENTURES™

SCOTT LOBDELL – Writer

TIM SMITH 3, PH MARCONDES – Artists

Based on the series by

FRANKLIN W. DIXON

PAPERCUTZ™

NEW YORK

TABLE OF CONTENTS

TABLE OF CONTENTS

THE HARDY BOYS ADVENTURES #2

"Abracadeath," "Dude Ranch O' Death!" "The Deadliest Stunt," and "Haley Danelle's Top Eight"

SCOTT LOBDELL – Writer
PH MARCONDES – Artist, "The Deadliest Stunt" "Dude Ranch O'Death!" "Haley Danelle's Top Eight"
TIM SMITH 3 – Artist, "Abracadeath"
MARK LERER – Letterer
LAURIE E. SMITH– Colorist
DIGIKORE – Colorist, "Abracadeath"
BIG BIRD ZATRYB – Production
SASHA KIMIATEK – Production Coordinator
JEFF WHITMAN – Assistant Managing Editor
JIM SALICRUP
Editor-in-Chief

ISBN: 978-1-62991-651-4

Printed in Korea
April 2017

Distributed by Macmillian
First Printing

"ABRACADEATH"
CHAPTER ONE:
"MAY I GET YOU SOME JUSTICE WITH THAT?"
WELCOME TO FRESH GROUNDS.
Y-YES. CAN YOU H-HELP ME?
I'M SURE WE CAN...

WHA -- ?!
IT'S OKAY, HEATHER--YOU'RE SAFE NOW!
LOOK OUT!
RUN!

... WE'LL START BY FREEING YOU FROM YOUR KIDNAPPER!
THE BIG JERK!
UHN!
POK

HOW DID YOU KNOW?!
ARE YOU KIDDING?
EVERY COP AND FEDERAL AGENT IN THE CITY IS LOOKING FOR YOU!
I GUESS THEY DIDN'T TELL YOU I WAS ARMED, EH?!
NO. AND THEY NEGLECTED TO TELL ME ABOUT YOUR BAD BREATH TOO.
LET ME OUT OF HERE!
HE'S GOT A GUN!
WE'LL SEE HOW FUNNY YOU ARE WITH A BULLET IN YOUR SMART MOUTH!
I'M GUESSING "NOT VERY."

KRASH

THUMP
THERE'S THAT COFFEE I ORDERED.

MAY I GET YOU SOME JUSTICE WITH THAT?

SERIOUSLY, WHEN I SAW THE GUN PRESSED AGAINST HEATHER'S BACK--

--I KNEW WE HAD TO ACT RIGHT AWAY.

I'M JUST GLAD WE WERE ABLE TO STOP THAT GUY BEFORE HE ADDED ANOTHER TEEN TO HIS LIST OF KIDNAP VICTIMS.
ALL IN A DAY'S WORK FOR AGENTS OF A.T.A.C...

...WHICH IS NO EXCUSE FOR NOT DOING OUR HOMEWORK.
I GET IT: "STUDY!"

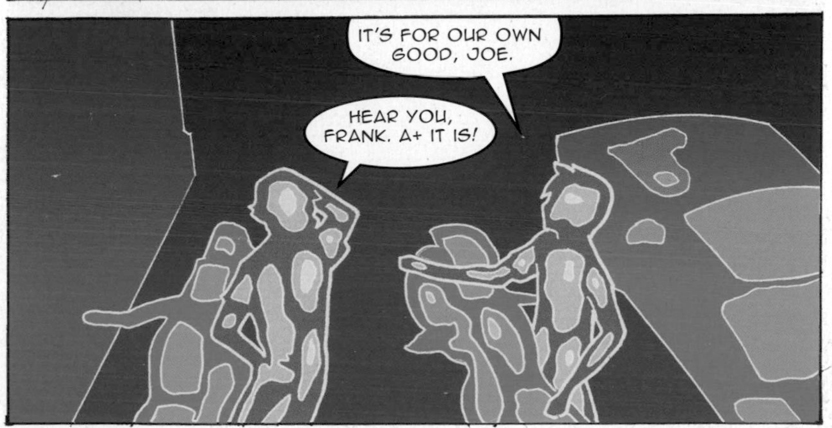
IT'S FOR OUR OWN GOOD, JOE.
HEAR YOU, FRANK. A+ IT IS!

CHAPTER TWO:
"THAT TRICK NEVER WORKS!"
NOW FOR MY FINAL ACT...I, DIA THE AMAZING, WILL PRODUCE A RABBIT OUT OF THIN AIR!
TAP TAP
BUT FIRST-- THE MAGIC WORDS!

ZOOLA BOOLA!
BAYPORT HIGH SCHOOL
BAYPORT TALENT SHOW!

SHE'S AWESOME-- ISN'T SHE?
AT THE VERY LEAST.

TO QUOTE A FAMOUS MAGICIANESS...
YNNUB RAEPPA!

CHT CHT?
LOOK-- IT'S HAPPY BUNNY!
WHERE'D HE COME FROM?!
SO CUTE!

THANK YOU VERY MUCH! YOU HAVE BEEN--
HA HA HO HA HEH HO HA!
LAUGHING? WHA--?

OH, NO!
BUNNYBOY, COME BACK!
?!
HOP!

HA HA!
HO HA!
BUNNYBOY--
HEEL! HEEL!
CRASH!
CLAP CLAP CLAP CLAP CLAP CLAP CLAP CLAP CLAP CLAP CLAP CLAP CLAP CLAP CLAP CLAP CLAP
SHE'S AS FUNNY AS DAZZLE!
WHAT A HOOT!
MAYBE YOU CAN MAKE YOURSELF DISAPPEAR NOW!
GET OFF THE STAGE, LOSER!

AT LEAST SHE'S TRYING, BRIAN!
WHY ARE YOU GIVING HER A HARD TIME!
WHAT'S IT TO YOU? I'M JUST TEASING HER.
AS GRATIFYING AS IT MIGHT BE TO CLEAN HIS CLOCK--
YOU'RE A.T.A.C. TRAINING GIVES YOU AN UNFAIR ADVANTAGE.
GRRRR
DID HE WHISPER TO YOU TO GIVE UP?! HA HA!
HE SAID IT'D BE TOO EASY.
WELL, WHAT DO WE HAVE HERE?

LOOK WHO I FOUND?
BUNNYBOY!
DIA'S GOING TO BE SO HAPPY!

MOMENTS LATER...
...BACKSTAGE...
CHEER UP, DIA.
CAN'T SNFF, SNFF BUNNYBOY IS GONE.

WHAT WERE THOSE MAGIC WORDS YOU USED: ZOOLA BOOLA?
BUNNYBOY! YOU'RE BACK!
CHT CHT

THANK YOU, JOE! YOU MUST HAVE LOOKED EVERYWHERE FOR HIM!
ACTUALLY...
THAT JOE, WHAT A GUY.

OH, WAIT--I JUST REMEMBERED SOMETHING.
I FOUND SOMETHING FOR YOU IN MY TOP HAT, BEFORE THE SHOW!

IT HAD YOUR NAMES ON IT. I CAN'T FIGURE OUT HOW IT GOT THERE.
UM... MAGIC?
ONE OF THE GAME CARTRIDGES A.T.A.C. USES TO GIVE US OUR CASES!

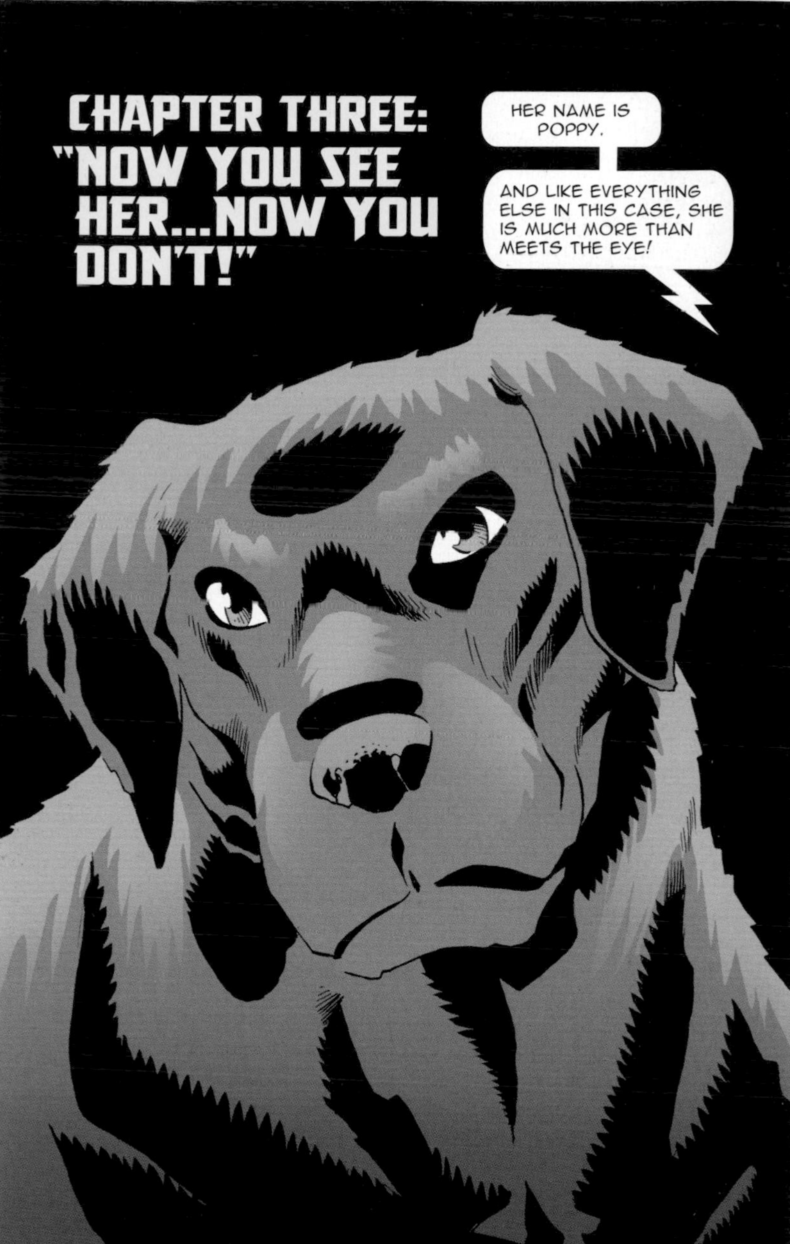
CHAPTER THREE: "NOW YOU SEE HER...NOW YOU DON'T!"
HER NAME IS POPPY.
AND LIKE EVERYTHING ELSE IN THIS CASE, SHE IS MUCH MORE THAN MEETS THE EYE!

WITH A CASE NAMED "ABRACADEATH" I WOULD IMAGINE SO.
SHUSH.

YOUR CASE BEGINS HERE, AT THE CASTLE MAGIQUE IN HOLLYWOOD!
IT IS A PRIVATE CLUB, ATTENDED BY THE WORLD'S GREATEST MAGICIANS!

MEMBERS COME FROM ALL OVER THE GLOBE IN ORDER TO PRACTICE AND PERFECT THEIR MAGIC SKILLS.

SOME HONE THEIR PSYCHIC SKILLS, LIKE KARNAQ OF THE MIDDLE EAST.

SOME, LIKE GLOM, SHUN TRADITION FOR THE MORE MODERN ART OF ILLUSION.

THEN THERE IS THE INCOMPARABLE CUTTING EDGE MAGICIAN, MISS TIQUE!
UM. SHE'S MY FAVORITE.

WITHOUT PEER, THE MOST RESPECTED OF ALL MAGICIANS...
...IS THE GREAT MARCONI!
IT IS HIS MISSING ASSISTANT, POPPY, THAT WE ARE ASKING YOU TO LOCATE BEFORE --

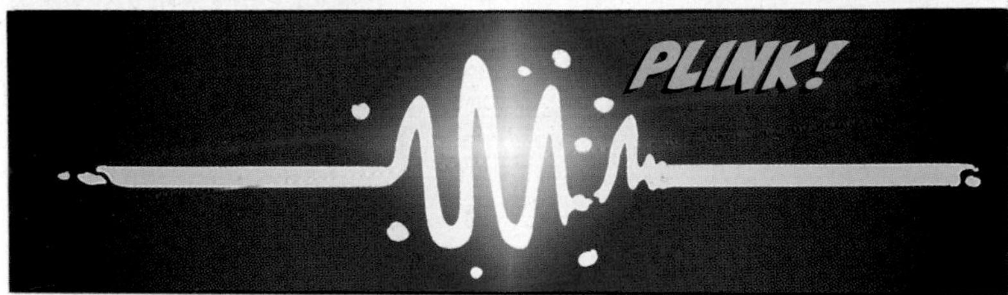
PLINK!

JOE--WHAT HAPPENED?
NOTHING. THE SCREEN JUST WENT BLANK!
NOW THE WHOLE SYSTEM HAS SHUT DOWN. EERIE.
CLICK CLICK

THIS IS ALL QUITE MYSTERIOUS.
HOW ARE WE SUPPOSED TO GET AN INVITE TO THE CASTLE MAGIQUE? LET ALONE HOW ARE WE SUPPOSED TO FIND POPPY?

JOE, FRANK!
YOU HAVE A VISITOR!

HEY--IT'S YOU! WHAT A SURPRISE.
HI! YOU'LL NEVER GUESS WHAT HAPPENED TO ME!
YOU MIGHT BE SURPRISED.

I JUST GOT THE MOST AMAZING THING DELIVERED TO MY DOOR!

AN INVITATION TO THE APPRENTICE'S WEEKEND AT THE CASTLE MAGIQUE--
--THIS WEEKEND!

NEED TO BRING TWO ASSISTANTS! AND SINCE YOU WERE SO GOOD WITH BUNNYBOY EARLIER...
MAGIC ISN'T SOME-THING ONE JUST JUMPS INTO BE--

OF COURSE, WE'LL COME! WE'LL BE HAPPY TO JOIN YOU!
OH, THANK YOU!
YOU TWO ROCK AND ROLL!
GREAT.

NOW, I'VE GOT A ZILLION THINGS TO DO BEFORE WE LEAVE TOMORROW!

WOW. THAT COULDN'T HAVE WORKED OUT BETTER IF WE HAD PLANNED IT.
ALMOST MAKES ONE A BELIEVER, HUH?

CHAPTER FOUR:
"ENTER FREELY AND OF YOUR OWN WILL!"
UM... UH... UM...

WELCOME...
...TO THE WORLD FAMOUS *CASTLE MAGIQUE!*

...

...I'VE BEEN WAITING MY ENTIRE LIFE TO BE HERE!

A MINUTE AGO YOU WERE TALL. NOW YOU'RE... WELL...

HOW DID YOU DO THAT?

HA! THE FIRST RULE OF THE CASTLE MAGIQUE...?

NOTHING IS AT IT APPEARS!

NOTHING!
FRANK! JOE! THAT BLACK SMOKE!
IS IT A FIRE?!
IT'S NOT BEHAVING LIKE REGULAR SMOKE.
HEAT RISES. THIS SMOKE IS CRAWLING ALONG THE FLOOR.
JUST IN CASE.
THAT SMALL TORNADO OF SMOKE?
IT'S MOVING AS IF IT'S ALIVE!

THE SMOKE IS NOT ALIVE.
BUT I AM... I, THE GREAT MARCONI!
WOW. YOU'RE EVERYTHING DIA SAID YOU WERE, AND MORE.
MAYBE SOMEDAY YOU CAN SHOW ME HOW YOU--
DON'T WASTE YOUR BREATH, FRANK: A MAGICIAN NEVER REVEALS HIS SECRETS!
ESPECIALLY NOT A LIVING LEGEND!
CLAP CLAP
CLAP CLAP

MR. GREAT MARCONI, SIR. IT IS AN HONOR TO MEET YOU AT LAST!
THE PLEASURE IS MINE, DEAR.
AND THERE'S NO "MR." IN FRONT OF GREAT MARCONI.

NOW IF...Y-YOU'LL COME...
JOE, QUICK-- A CHAIR!
HIS PUPILS ARE DIALATED, HE'S OUT OF BREATH.

HERE YOU GO, SIR!
TH-THANK YOU, YOUNG MAN.
THE GREAT MARCONI THANKS YOU.

WE WERE HAPPIEST WHEN WE WERE GIVING FREE SHOWS FOR HOSPITALS AND ORPHANAGES ACROSS THE WORLD.

I KEEP HOPING SHE'LL JUST POP UP! SOME SUSPECT FOUL PLAY, BUT THERE WAS NO RANSOM DEMAND!

NOW ENOUGH ABOUT ME.
I HAVE AN APPRENTICE TO INSTRUCT.
AND AS POPPY HERSELF WOULD SAY--"THE SHOW MUST GO ON!"

WE HAVE A FEW MOMENTS TO TALK IN PRIVATE.
NOW WE KNOW WHY A.T.A.C. WANTS US INVOLVED. ALL THOSE KIDS THAT BENEFITED FROM HIS FREE SHOWS.

HE'S PUTTING ON A BRAVE FRONT, BUT HIS HEART IS BROKEN.
YOU THINK IT MIGHT HAVE BEEN ONE OF THE OTHER MAGICIANS WHO TOOK HIS DOG-- TO STIFLE THE COMPETITION?

FRANK AND JOE HARDY!
WHO--?
WHAT, FRANK? YOU DON'T RECOGNIZE THE VOICE...?

IT'S TRE* GELBMAN, THE WRITER WE MET ON THE BULLET TRAIN!
WHY AM I NOT SURPRISED TO FIND YOU TWO KNEE DEEP IN A MYSTERY?
*SEE HARDY BOYS ADVENTURES #1.

NOT THAT I MIND. LAST TIME YOU TWO CAME IN HANDY!
MORE THAN ONCE.

THOUGH, I GUESS IT'S POSSIBLE YOU TWO ARE BAD LUCK MAGNETS.
HOW DO WE EXPLAIN WITHOUT TELLING HER ABOUT A.T.A.C.?
BUT ENOUGH ABOUT US, TRE...

ROOOOOOOOOAAAR!

GRRRROWL

DON'T WORRY, TRE. THIS IS JUST AN ILLUSION.
NO WAY A LION IS RUNNING LOOSE IN THE BUILDING.

THEN AGAIN.
SLASH

CHAPTER FIVE:
"CLAWS FOR CONCERN!"
IT IS REAL, I-ISN'T I-IT?
KEEP BEHIND US AND STAY CALM.
DON'T LOSE YOUR HEAD, TRE.
OKAY, BAD CHOICE OF WORDS.

R-REAL?
GET DOWN HERE YOU'RE SAFE FOR NOW.
WHAT DO WE DO?
ON THE COUNT OF THREE, I'LL DISTRACT HIM. YOU RUN.
ONE...
TWO...
ROAR

FWOOSH!
USE THIS TORCH FROM THE WALL--THAT SHOULD KEEP HIM BACK LONG ENOUGH FOR US TO GET OUT OF HERE.
QUICK THINKING, JOE!
BUT IS IT ME, OR--
--DOES HE LOOK... SCARED?
I KNOW JUST HOW HE FEELS.

--TO TRY TO INCINERATE MY STAR ATTRACTION. THOUGH I UNDERSTAND YOUR FEAR.

WAS LITTLE KITTY SCARED?

SCRTCH SCRTCH

I HAD NO SOONER ARRIVED TO FEED MY FURRY FRIEND WHEN I DISCOVERED HE WAS MISSING.
SOMEHOW HIS CAGE WAS OPENED.

KITTY WOULD NOT BE THE FIRST STAGE ACT THAT HAS GONE MISSING OF LATE.
NOW WITHOUT ANOTHER WORD, WE AWAY.

THESE ARE NOT YOUR AVERAGE EVERYDAY PEOPLE AROUND HERE.
YOU NOTICED?
WE HAVE TO EXPECT THE UNEXPECTED.

LATER, ON THE GRAND STAGE...
THIS IS WHERE DIA WANTED HER TRUNK.
ULP!
I'LL WALK YOU TO YOUR ROOM, TRE-- TO MAKE SURE YOU GET THERE SAFELY.
ALWAYS THE GENTLEMAN.
AS DIA'S ASSISTANT, I SHOULD MAKE SURE EVERYTHING IS IN PLACE FOR HER CLASSES.

HEY THERE, BUNNYBOY!
DO YOU KNOW HOW HAPPY I AM TO SEE YOU?
CHT CHT

YEP, EXACTLY THAT AMOUNT!
NOW I KNOW WHY MAGICIANS LIKE TO PERFORM WITH ANIMALS.
BECAUSE THEY ARE SO CUTE!

I KNOW WHY YOU ARE HERE, JOE HARDY!
HUNH?
YOU AND YOUR BROTHER FRANK!

I KNOW YOU ARE SHOCKED--SHOCKED BY THE MENTAL MIGHT OF KARNAQ!
BUT WHO ELSE BUT I WOULD KNOW THAT YOU ARE DOING THE BIDDING OF... L.I.L.A.C.?
TICTACS?
ISN'T THAT A BREATH MINT OR SOMETHING?

CLEVER. BUT NONE CAN HIDE THE TRUTH FROM KARNAQ!

EVEN NOW I AM GETTING A PSYCHIC IMAGE OF THE MISSING DOG.
SHE'S ALONE, SAD. BUT SHE HAS FOOD AND WATER.
I CANNOT SENSE WHERE SHE IS... BUT SHE IS SAFE.

NEXT I WILL TRY TO-- ARRRRRGH!
KARNAQ! SIR, WHAT'S WRONG?!
DO NOT WORRY ABOUT ME! I WAS OVERCOME BY A PSYCHIC CALL FOR HELP!
IT WAS YOUR BROTHER... QUICKLY, GO TO HIM! THE BASEMENT!
I'M NOT CONVINCED YOU'RE NOT SCAMMING ME, KARNAQ.
BUT I CAN'T TAKE THAT RISK, CAN I?

THERE IT IS--UP AHEAD!
FRANK! ARE YOU DOWN HERE?!
GASP!

CHAPTER SIX:
"H_2OH!"
FRANK?! CAN YOU HEAR ME?!
DON'T WORRY-- I'LL GET YOU OUT OF THERE!

POUND! POUND!
THE GLASS IS SO THICK AND THE TOP IS LOCKED!
AND HE'S RUNNING OUT OF AIR!
NEED SOMETHING HARD LIKE...
THAT LOOSE STONE!
STAND BACK, FRANK! THAT TANK IS AS GOOD AS...
?!

?!
EMPTY?
BUT... HOW?

I HEARD YOU CALLING ME.
AND, WHY ARE YOU GOING TO SMASH THAT TANK?

FRANK!
JOE?

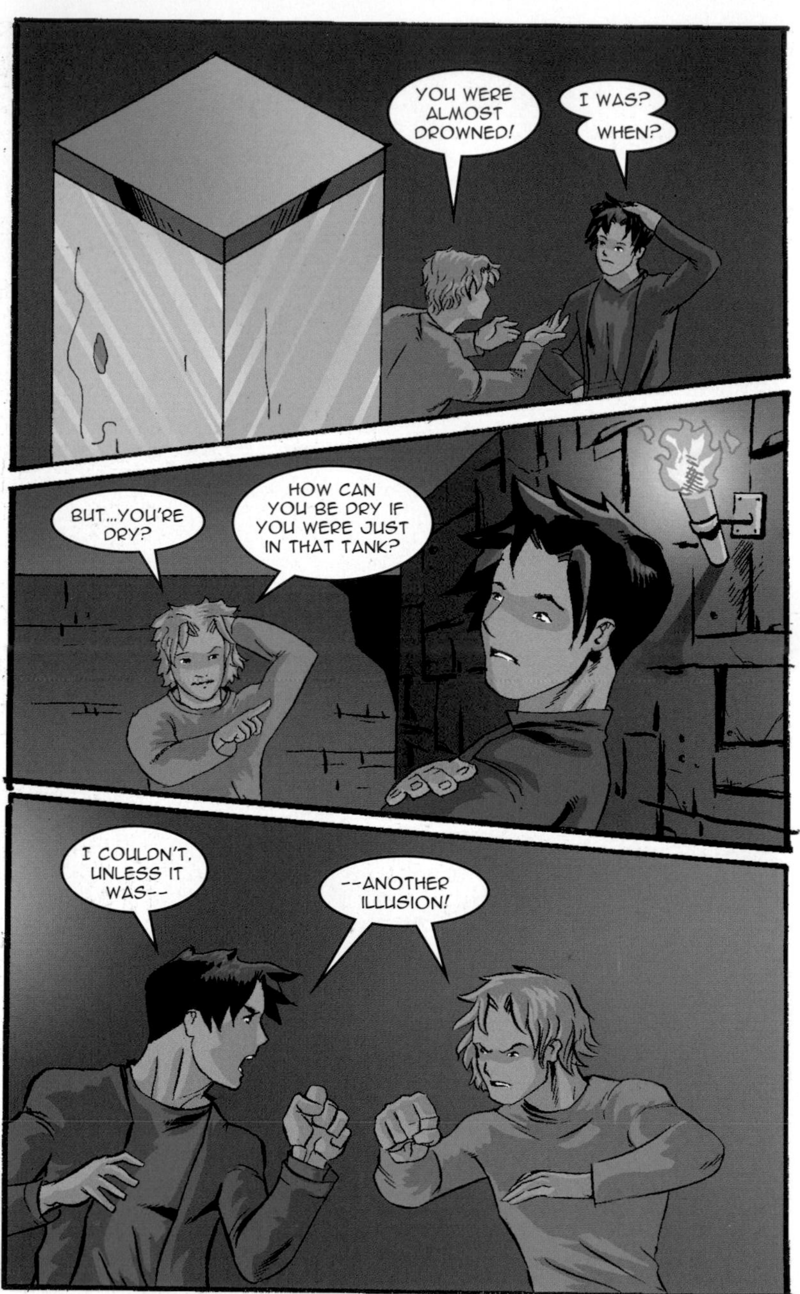
YOU WERE ALMOST DROWNED!
I WAS?
WHEN?
BUT...YOU'RE DRY?
HOW CAN YOU BE DRY IF YOU WERE JUST IN THAT TANK?
I COULDN'T. UNLESS IT WAS--
--ANOTHER ILLUSION!

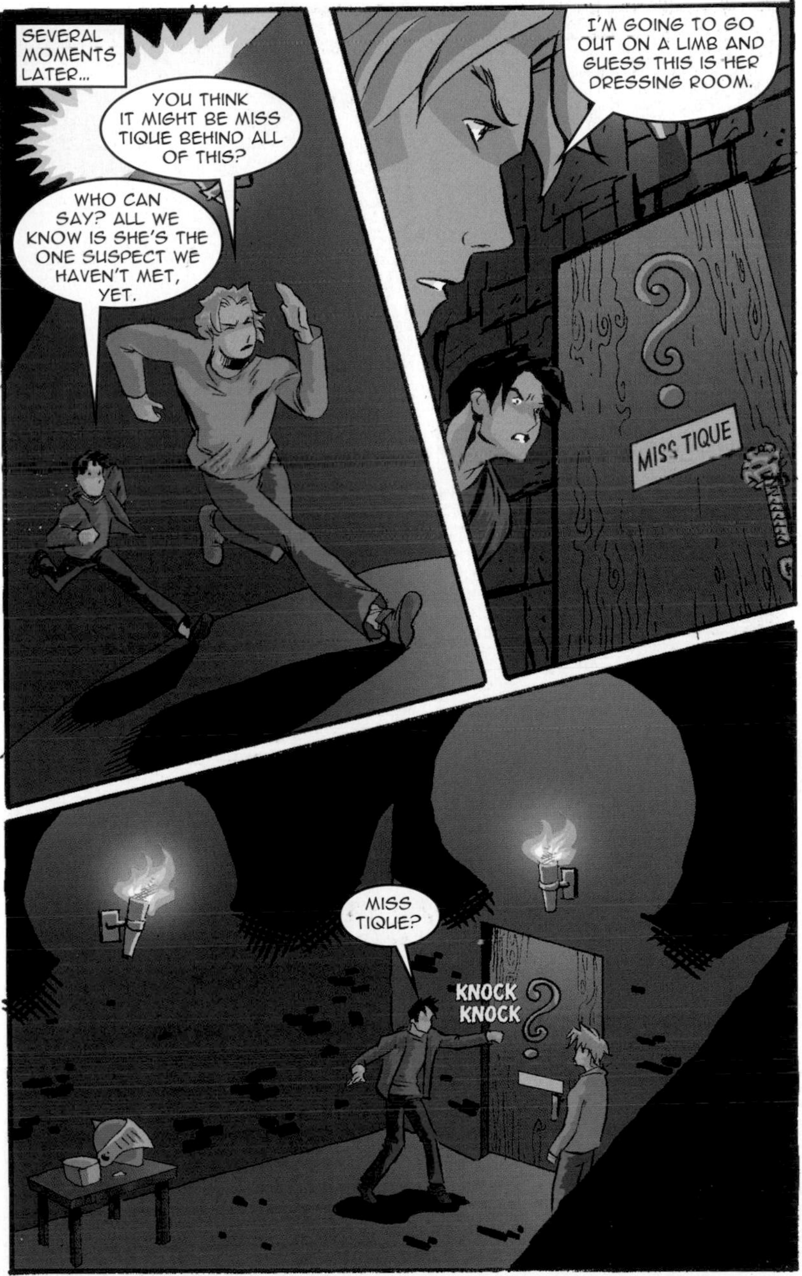
SEVERAL MOMENTS LATER...
YOU THINK IT MIGHT BE MISS TIQUE BEHIND ALL OF THIS?
WHO CAN SAY? ALL WE KNOW IS SHE'S THE ONE SUSPECT WE HAVEN'T MET, YET.
I'M GOING TO GO OUT ON A LIMB AND GUESS THIS IS HER DRESSING ROOM.
MISS TIQUE
MISS TIQUE?
KNOCK KNOCK

ENTER.
HOW MAY I HELP YOU?
AN AUTOGRAPH, PERHAPS?
WE'RE NOT FAN BOYS. WE WERE HERE HELPING OUR FRIEND DIA.
BUT WE ARE CURIOUS AS TO POPPY'S WHEREABOUTS. IF YOU CAN THINK OF ANY-THING THAT MIGHT BE HELPFUL?

EH?
TAP TAP
TAP TAP
EXCUSE ME, BOYS...?

MISS TIQUE?
CAN YOU TELL ME WHY YOU'RE HERE--TALKING TO YOURSELVES?
HOW ARE YOU OUT HERE IN THE HALLWAY WHEN--

--YOU'RE IN YOUR... DRESSING ROOM?
SHE'S NOT. SHE'S GONE.
IF SHE WAS EVER THERE AT ALL.

LET'S TRY THIS AGAIN!

CREEEEEEAK

MISS TIQUE?

HELLO?

CHAPTER SEVEN:
"WE ARE LEGION!"
HELLO. CAN WE HELP YOU?
SHE'S GOOD.

HELLO. CAN WE HELP YOU?
HELLO. CAN WE HELP YOU?

EXCUSE ME?! CAN I HELP YOU?
WANT TO TAKE A GUESS WHO THAT IS?
IT CAN ONLY BE--

MISS TIQUE! I ASSUME YOU KNOW WHOSE DRESSING ROOM YOU'RE STANDING IN!
WITHOUT MY PERMISSION I SHOULD HASTEN TO ADD!

JOE, THERE'S NOBODY IN THE DRESSING ROOM. IS THERE?
THAT WOULD BE A "NO."

HMP.
IMAGINE THAT.

I'M SORRY, MA'AM. I HAVE TO ASK...HOW DID YOU PULL OFF THAT ILLUSION JUST NOW?
AND I JUST HAVE TO SAY...A MAGICIAN NEVER REVEALS HER SECRETS.

BUT JUST THIS ONCE, I WILL TELL YOU IT IS DONE WITH MIRRORS.
YOU SEE THIS ONE HERE IS ATTACHED TO A HINGE THAT--

IIIIIIIIIIIIIIIIIEEEEEEEEEEEEEEE!
THAT SCREAM! IT'S--
--DIA!
THAT DOESN'T SURPRISE ME. BUT WE HAVE TO HELP OUR FRIEND.
THE SCREAMING STOPPED! I HOPE SHE'S OKAY!
IT CAME FROM THE UPPER FLOORS! THERE'S THE STAIRWELL--

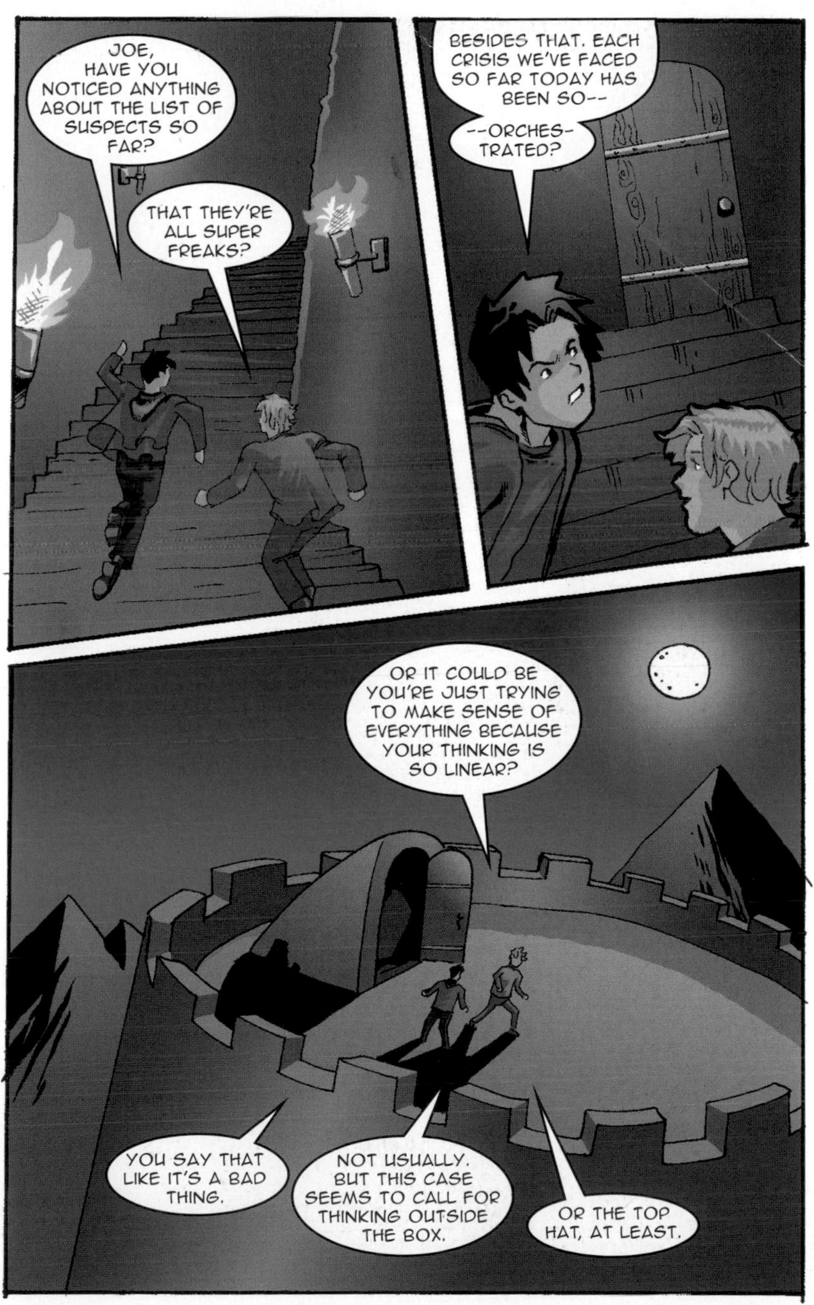
JOE, HAVE YOU NOTICED ANYTHING ABOUT THE LIST OF SUSPECTS SO FAR?
THAT THEY'RE ALL SUPER FREAKS?
BESIDES THAT. EACH CRISIS WE'VE FACED SO FAR TODAY HAS BEEN SO--
--ORCHES-TRATED?
OR IT COULD BE YOU'RE JUST TRYING TO MAKE SENSE OF EVERYTHING BECAUSE YOUR THINKING IS SO LINEAR?
YOU SAY THAT LIKE IT'S A BAD THING.
NOT USUALLY. BUT THIS CASE SEEMS TO CALL FOR THINKING OUTSIDE THE BOX.
OR THE TOP HAT, AT LEAST.

JOE! FRANK! PLEASE! YOU HAVE TO DO SOMETHING!
CHT CHT
CALM DOWN, DIA--YOU'RE SAFE NOW.
WHAT'S WRONG... WHY WERE YOU SCREAMING?

CHAPTER EIGHT:
"HAVE I MADE MY POINT?!"
I WENT TO GET A GLASS OF WATER.
WHEN I C-CAME BACK... I FOUND HIM LIKE TH-THAT?
WHAT A HORRIBLE WAY TO DIE.
DIA, JOE AND I NEED TO EXAMINE THE BODY FOR CLUES. STAY HERE WITH BUNNYBOY.

SHOULD WE CALL AN AMBULANCE? COULD HE STILL BE ALIVE?
WITH THOSE INJURIES? I DON'T SEE HOW IT'S POSSIBLE.

WHAT--?!?
YOU STARTLED ME! WHAT ARE YOU TWO BOYS DOING UP HERE?!

YOU WERE JUST PRACTICING ANOTHER TRICK?
MY LATEST!
I CALL IT "MARCONI SHISH-KA-BOB!"
IT'S CERTAINLY A SHOW-STOPPER.

MR. GREAT MARCONI! YOU'RE ALIVE! I WAS SO SCARED!
I'M SORRY I DIDN'T HEAR YOU APPROACHING.
THE OLDER I GET THE MORE I DEPEND UPON MY HEARING AID. LET ME ADJUST IT.
I'M SORRY I LEAD YOU TO BELIEVE OTHER-WISE, YOUNG LADY.
EVER SINCE POPPY WAS DOGNAPPED, I'M AFRAID I HAVEN'T BEEN IN TOP FORM.
I'VE BEEN DISTRACTED, LISTLESS.
HMMM.

IT IS GOING TO TAKE SOME TIME. YOU TWO WERE VERY CLOSE.
YOU DON'T UNDERSTAND. MY WHOLE LIFE WAS MY ACT.

I EVEN NEGLECTED MY OWN FAMILY FOR YEARS.
IN MANY WAYS, POPPY BECAME THE LITTLE GIRL I HAD FOOLISHLY ABANDONED FOR MY CAREER.

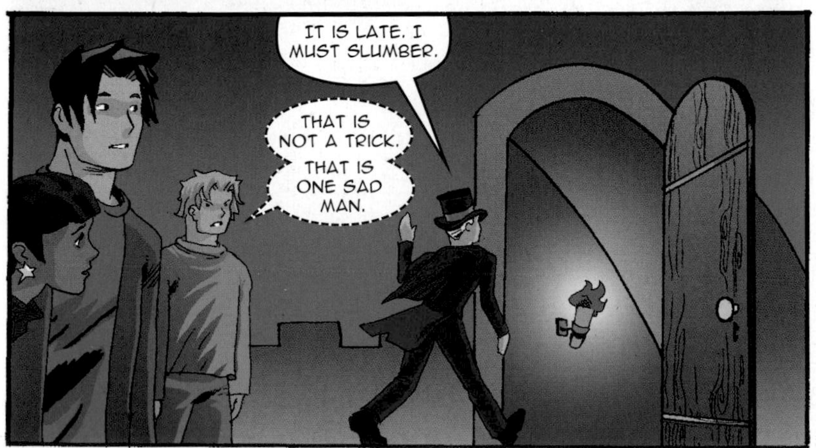
IT IS LATE. I MUST SLUMBER.
THAT IS NOT A TRICK.
THAT IS ONE SAD MAN.

JOE...WHEN IS AN ILLUSION NOT AN ILLUSION?
HM. THAT'S A PUZZLER.
WAIT--I GET IT!
WHEN IT'S NOT AN ILLUSION AT ALL!
UM, GUYS?
BUNNYBOY?

SO FAR EVERYTHING WE'VE SEEN HERE HAS JUST BEEN A DEFLECTION.
AN ATTEMPT TO DISTRACT US FROM THE JOB OF FINDING POPPY.
EVERYTHING HAS BEEN STAGED. DOWN TO THE SMALLEST DETAIL.
BUT THE ONE THING THESE PURVEYORS OF MAGIC DIDN'T COUNT ON...
...WAS THE PRESENCE OF TRE GELBMAN, THE WRITER. THIS IS HER ROOM...
SHE'S GONE! BUT WHERE?!

AND SINCE THERE'S NO WAY POPPY WROTE THAT LETTER...

SOMEONE ELSE WANTED HER HERE TO STAGE A REUNION.

MOMENTS LATER THE HARDY BOYS RACE TOWARDS THE MAIN THEATRE!

TRE--ARE YOU HERE?!
WE FIGURED OUT WHAT'S--

FRANK, WHY DO I GET THE FEELING THAT'S NOT AN ILLUSION WE'RE LOOKING AT?
BECAUSE... IT ISN'T!

CHAPTER NINE:
"FLAME! I WANT TO LIVE FOREVER!"
THESE FLAMES ARE REAL! AND THE ROPES!
PLEASE HELP ME!

I'LL GO FIND A FIRE EXTIN-GUISHER!
HURRY! I'LL TRY TO GET HER OUT OF THERE!
THOUGH TO BE HONEST, I'M AT A LOSS AS TO HOW.
I'M A LOT OF THINGS, BUT NOT FIREPROOF.
FRANK, THERE'S NO W-WAY TO SAVE ME...IS THERE?
THERE'S ALWAYS A WAY, TRE.
ALWAYS.

WE JUST NEED TO FIND A ROUTE TO--
WUFF! WUFF!
HUH?!
IS THAT... BARKING?
POPPY?!
WUFF! WUFF!
AAAAROOOOOOO!

GOOD GIRL!
UM, FRANK? I'M HAPPY TO SEE HER TOO, BUT--
--YOU MIGHT WANT TO PRIORITIZE YOUR RESCUES!

TRUST ME.
I AM!
YOU WEREN'T BARKING TO GET SAVED!
YOU WERE SHOWING ME THE WAY TO SAVE TRE!
WUFF! WUFF!

I FOUND THIS FIRE EXTINGUISHER IN AN EMERGENCY STAIRWELL!
I HAVE TO SPRAY THE STAGE WITH WATER, TRE-- SO DUCK!
OKAY, I'M--
YANK!
THOSE ARE SOME MAD DUCKING SKILLS.
SPWOOSH!

FRANK! YOU SAVED ME!
WUFF! WUFF!
THAT'S RIGHT, POPPY-- WE RESCUED HER TOGETHER.
NOW LETS GET YOU UNTIED AND OUT OF HERE.
I GUESS I OWE YOU ANOTHER THANK YOU, FRANK.
WIFF! WIFF!
YES! YES, OKAY POPPY--A BIG THANK YOU TO YOU TOO!
IS IT ME--OR DOES THAT LOOK A LOT LIKE A LONG LOST REUNION?

IN A LITTLE BIT...
YOU TWO HAVE GOTTEN SO GOOD AT SAVING MY LIFE--
--MY NEXT BOOK IS GOING TO BE CALLED *THE HARDY BOYS, UNDERCOVER BROTHERS.*
HA. GOOD ONE.

JOE, DO YOU SEE HOW EXCITED POPPY IS TO SEE TRE?
YEAH? THAT'S HOW DOGS ARE WHENEVER THEY SEE AN OLD FRIEND OR A MEMBER OF...
YIP! YIP!

CHAPTER TEN:
"AND THE KILLER IS...! (OR ISN'T!)"
THANK YOU ALL FOR COMING.
I KNEW YOU WERE GOING TO SAY THAT.
SHUT UP, KARNAQ.
WE JUST WANT TO GET TO THE BOTTOM OF THIS ONCE AND FOR ALL.
IT IS ALL FOR NAUGHT WITHOUT MY BELOVED POPPY.

WE ALL ASSUMED POPPY WAS KIDNAPPED BY A FELLOW MAGICIAN--
--AS A MEANS OF FORCING YOU INTO RETIREMENT.
BUT IN A CASTLE WHERE ILLUSION REIGNS, NO ONE IS QUITE WHO THEY APPEAR TO BE.
THAT INCLUDES THE KIDNAP VICTIM.
WHAT ARE YOU SAYING?

AS YOU MIGHT SAY...
"TA DA!"
YIP! YIP!

POPPY!
YIPE! YIPE!
WUFF! WUFF!

HOW'D YOU DO IT, GUYS?! HOW DID YOU FREE POPPY?
LAP LAP LAP

MORE IMPORTANTLY--WHO IS THE PERSON RESPONSIBLE FOR TAKING HER AWAY FROM ME IN THE FIRST PLACE?
WHO WOULD DARE PUT MY BELOVED DOG AT RISK?!
WHEN WE SAW POPPY'S REACTION IT WAS CLEAR TO US SHE KNEW TRE.
THERES NO EASY WAY TO SAY THIS...
IT WAS *YOU!*
WHA--?!
THAT'S ABSURD!

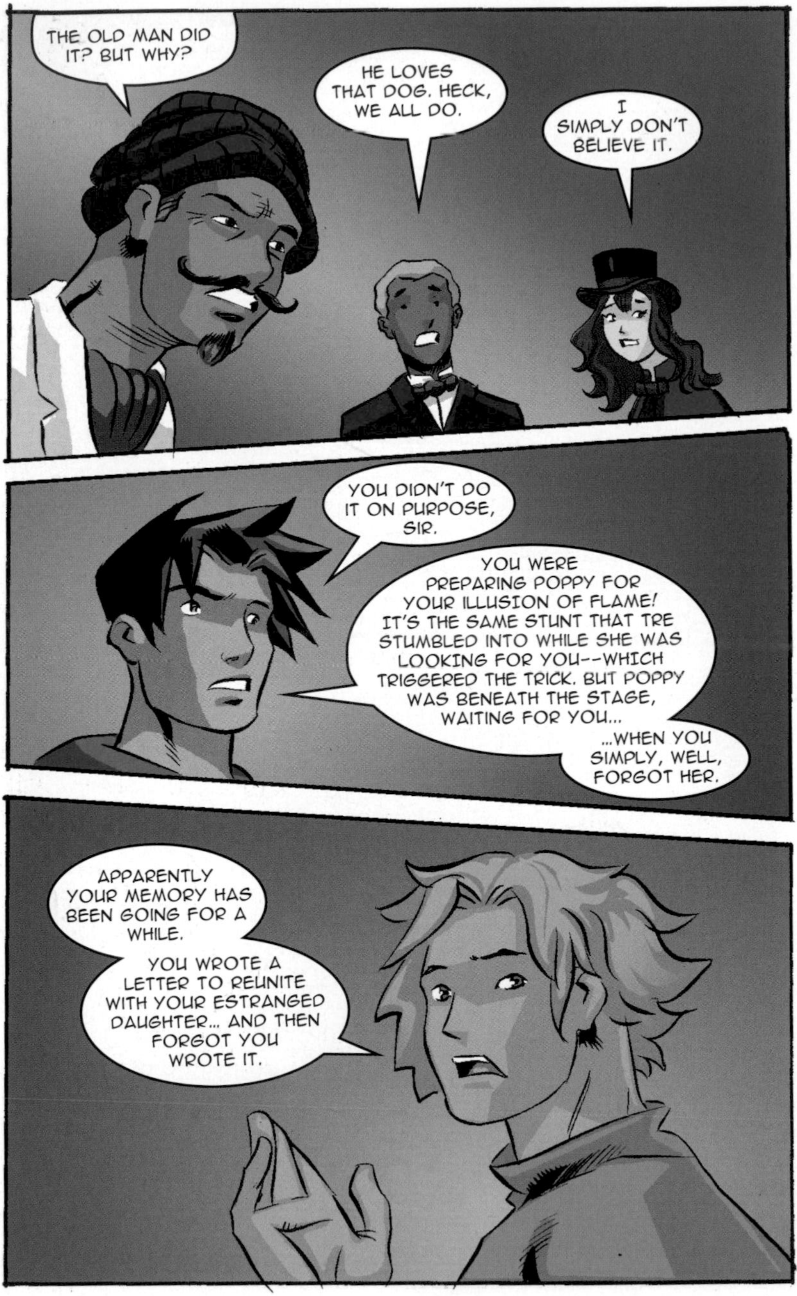

THE OLD MAN DID IT? BUT WHY?

HE LOVES THAT DOG. HECK, WE ALL DO.

I SIMPLY DON'T BELIEVE IT.

YOU DIDN'T DO IT ON PURPOSE, SIR.

YOU WERE PREPARING POPPY FOR YOUR ILLUSION OF FLAME! IT'S THE SAME STUNT THAT TRE STUMBLED INTO WHILE SHE WAS LOOKING FOR YOU--WHICH TRIGGERED THE TRICK. BUT POPPY WAS BENEATH THE STAGE, WAITING FOR YOU...

...WHEN YOU SIMPLY, WELL, FORGOT HER.

THANK YOU SO MUCH, GENTLEMEN.
IT WAS AN HONOR.
WE'RE GLAD TO SEE THE TWO OF YOU REUNITED.
YOU MEAN THE THREE OF US!
WUPF!

FOR MY NEXT TRICK, I NEED A VOLUNTEER FROM THE AUDIENCE.
PREFERABLY SOMEONE WHO IS HANDSOME BUT NOT VERY BRIGHT!
CHAPTER ELEVEN: "AT NO TIME DO MY FINGERS LEAVE MY HAND!"

PICK ME! I'M VERY HANDSOME!
PERFECT!

THIS IS CERTAINLY SOME SHOW SHE'S PUTTING ON.
SHE CAME A LONG WAY WORKING WITH THE GREAT MARCONI.

NOW CLOSE YOUR EYES AND THINK--AS HARD AS THAT MAY BE.
MAGINE THE MOST HORRIFYING THING YOU CAN.
BRRRR.

AAAAAAAAAAAAH!
TA DA!
AMAZING!
THAT HAS TO BE AN ILLUSION... RIGHT?
IT'S GOT TO BE... RIGHT?
WOOHOO!
THE END... RIGHT?

YOU'RE NAME IS LEAH, RIGHT?
RMPH!
MY NAME IS JOE HARDY.
I'LL HAVE YOU OUT OF HERE IN A MOMENT...
"DUDE RANCH O'DEATH!"

...OR SOONER!
IIIIIIIEEEEEE!
LOOK OUT!
HOW DID
SHE GET THERE?!

CHAPTER ONE: "RIGHT TRACK, WRONG TRACK!"

OULPHN!
PRMP PHLPHN!
I AGREE: THAT WAS CLOSE!
BLUNK!
OKAY, YOU'RE FREE.
WE HAVE TO WORK TOGETHER TO GET DOWN BEFORE THAT ROLLER COASTER RETURNS.
TOO LATE, JOE HARDY--IT'S COMING BACK!
YEAH. I SEE.
I'M SURE HE'S BUSY, BUT I HAVE TO WONDER--

"--WHAT MY BROTHER IS UP TO RIGHT NOW?"
CLANG!
IF YOU'RE GOING TO KILL ME BEFORE I STOP YOU, YOU'RE GOING TO HAVE TO TRY A LITTLE HARDER. SIR.
SMART MOUTH! YOU'LL NEVER REACH THAT ROLLER COASTER EMERGENCY BRAKE IN TIME!
WHA--?!
AS A WISE MAN ONCE SAID --
--NEVER SAY NEVER!

TAKE MY HAND, LEAH. ON THE COUNT OF THREE,WE'RE GOING TO JUMP TO ANOTHER TRACK.
NO! I C-CAN'T!
MY FOOT IS STUCK--I CAN'T GET IT OUT!
DON'T WORRY--I'LL GET YOU OUT.
YOU C-CAN'T! JOE, IT'S TOO LATE!

P-PLEASE--
YOU HAVE TO
JUMP.
SAVE
YOURSELF!
STAY CALM.
A LOT CAN
HAPPEN IN TEN
SECONDS.
SCREEE!
ZPRITZ!
THE BRAKES!
SOMEONE
STOPPED US!
SCREEEEECH!
BUT WILL IT
STOP BEFORE IT
REACHES US?!
I VOTE
YES.

YES! WE'RE SAFE!

DUDE!

YOU MUST HAVE A GUARDIAN ANGEL!

MAYBE. BUT WHAT I KNOW I HAVE...

"...IS A BROTHER I CAN COUNT ON!"

IN A WORD: PHEW!

LATER, AS THE CULPRIT IS TAKEN INTO CUSTODY...
FRANK, JOE, THANK YOU FOR LOCATING AND RESCUING THE GOVERNOR'S DAUGHTER.
JUST DOING OUR PART, SIR.
AND, HEY, IT WAS FUN, TOO.
FBI
SPEAKING OF FUN, I'D LIKE TO THANK YOU PERSONALLY IN THE TUNNEL OF LOVE!
MAYBE SOME OTHER TIME?
HA! I DON'T KNOW WHY HE'S SO SURPRISED. THIS ALWAYS HAPPENS TO HIM!

CHAPTER TWO: "HAPPY TRAILS... OF DOOM!"
SO IF IT WEREN'T FOR THE VISION OF PRESIDENT THOMAS JEFFERSON, MERIWETHER LEWIS AND WILLIAM CLARK WOULD CERTAINLY NOT HAVE BECOME FAMOUS AS LEWIS AND CLARK--
--THE GREATEST EXPLORERS OF EARLY AMERICA.

...AND THAT CONCLUDES MY REPORT ON LEWIS AND CLARK.

SPLENDID, NESTOR. EXCELLENT JOB.

I GOT ONE!
DID THEY DISCOVER THE PORTABLE TOILET, TOO?!
HEH HEH
HA!

UM...UH...UM.
I-I DON'T KNOW...I D-DON'T THINK SO.
UH...

IGNORE BRIAN CONRAD...
...HE'S WAITING FOR SOMEONE TO INVENT A PORTABLE BRAIN.
HA HA!
CONRAD GOT OWNED!
GOOD ONE!

BRRRING!

BAYPORT
HIGH SCHOOL

WHERE DO YOU GET OFF EMBARRASSING ME IN FRONT OF THE WHOLE CLASS?
I COULDN'T HAVE DONE IT IF YOU HADN'T HELPED BY OPENING YOUR MOUTH.
HA HA!
ZING!
I'VE HAD ENOUGH OF YOU, FRANK HARDY.
MEET ME IN THE EMPTY LOT ACROSS THE STREET AFTER SCHOOL.
HONESTLY, I'D BE HAPPY TO...
...BUT I'VE BEEN TRAINED FOR HAND-TO-HAND COMBAT BY THE AMERICAN TEENS AGAINST CRIME.*
BRIAN WOULDN'T LAST TWO SECONDS.
*OR A.T.A.C., FOR SHORT.

BE THERE, HARDY!
DON'T MAKE ME COME LOOKING FOR YOU, COWARD!
OOO!
HE DIDN'T!

S-SORRY I CAUSED THIS. I KN-KNOW YOU WERE JUST DEFENDING ME IN CLASS.
DON'T WORRY ABOUT IT, NESTOR.

YOU DIDN'T MAKE BRIAN A JERK--HE WAS BORN THAT WAY.
JOIN ME FOR LUNCH, NESTOR?
S-SURE! OF COURSE!

...AND EVERYONE KNOWS HOW MUCH I LOVE MILKSHAKES!

OH, ALEX SIMMONS-- YOU'RE TOO FUNNY!

HA HA!

HEY, JOE-- GRAB A SEAT!

I'D LOVE TO, ALEX. BUT I JUST CAME TO GET FRANK.

I NEED SOME HELP ON A PROJECT.

I'LL CATCH YOU GUYS LATER. AND NESTOR--

--GREAT JOB ON THAT REPORT!

THANKS, FRANK!

Audio Visual Department
SORRY TO PULL YOU AWAY FROM LUNCH, FRANK--
--BUT WHEN THIS GAME DISC SHOWED UP IN MY LOCKER, I FIGURED IT WAS IMPORTANT.
IT'S HOW A.T.A.C. GIVES US OUR CASES.
AND THIS ONE "DUDE RANCH O' DEATH" SEEMS PRETTY CRYPTIC.

WELCOME, HARDY BOYS. AMERICAN TEENS AGAINST CRIME THANK YOU FOR THE SERVICE TO YOUR COUNTRY THAT YOU ARE ABOUT TO PROVIDE.

A.T.A.C.

"THIS CASE TAKES PLACE IN THE STATE OF NEVADA--

"--WHERE MUCH OF THE COUNTRYSIDE RETAINS ITS NATURAL WILDERNESS.

"THIS IS THE PERFECT PLACE FOR SORROW RANCH--

"--A RESIDENTIAL PROGRAM FOR TROUBLED TEENS.

SORROW RANCH

"THE FACILITY IS AN ALTERNATIVE TO JAIL OR A HALFWAY HOUSE FOR TEENAGERS WHO HAVE HAD TROUBLE WITH THE LAW.

"FAR FROM THEIR CITY HOMES, IN A NATURAL ENVIRONMENT, THEY LEARN HOW TO RIDE HORSES...

"...AND, JUST AS IMPORTANT, HOW TO CLEAN UP AFTER THEM.

"IT BUILDS CHARACTER.

"RECENTLY, HOWEVER, SEVERAL TEENS HAVE GONE MISSING FROM THE PROGRAM.
"WE CAN'T HELP BUT SUSPECT FOUL PLAY."

IT SURE LOOKS THAT WAY TO ME.
WHAT HAPPENED TO "SHUSH"?

"DENNIS HOGAN, THE 'WARDEN' AT SORROW RANCH IS A FAIR BUT FIRM MAN.
"HE TAKES HIS RESPONSIBILITY TO HIS CHARGES VERY SERIOUSLY.

"MARY STROM IS IN CHARGE OF THE DAY-TO-DAY RUNNING OF THE HOUSE AND FARM.
"SHE BRINGS MUCH WARMTH AND AFFECTION TO HER JOB.

"JUAN BARR IS A TOUGH MAN FOR A TOUGH JOB.
"HE IS BOTH A GUARD AND AN INSTRUCTOR.

"VIOLET TREMMEL AND SAM WORETH ARE THE ONLY CURRENT KIDS WHO WERE THERE--

"--DURING THE MOST RECENT DISAPPEARANCES OF THEIR FELLOW TROUBLED TEENS.

"THESE TECHNOLOGICALLY REDESIGNED PIECES OF WESTERN GEAR WILL BE WAITING FOR YOU UPON YOUR ARRIVAL AT SORROW RANCH.

"NOW MOVE ALONG, LITTLE DOGGIES.
"AND GOOD LUCK."
CLICK
A DUDE RANCH? IF NOT FOR THE MISSING TEENS, THIS WOULD BE FUN.

I AGREE. BUT WHAT ABOUT OUR COVER STORY?
WHAT KIND OF TROUBLE COULD ONE OF US GET INTO THAT WOULD LAND US AT SORROW RANCH?
HMMM.

IN THE LOT ACROSS THE STREET, AFTER SCHOOL...
SO THERE YOU ARE, HARDY! I FIGURED YOU'D BE TOO SCARED TO SHOW YOUR FACE AROUND--
WHAM!
THAT'S CERTAINLY ONE WAY TO DO IT.
18

CHAPTER THREE: "HOWDY, PARTNER... NOW DIE!"
ONE COURT APPEARANCE LATER...
...AND A JUDGE WORKING WITH A.T.A.C. HAS SENTENCED FRANK HARDY TO A WEEK AT--
SORROW RANCH!
EVERYBODY OFF!

STEP OFF THE BUS IN AN ORDERLY FASHION.
KEEP AN OPEN MIND AND AN OPEN HEART...

...AND YOU MIGHT EVEN ENJOY YOURSELVES.
MAYBE.

STAND AT ATTENTION, YOU--YOU CITY-SLICKERS!
OR MAYBE NOT.

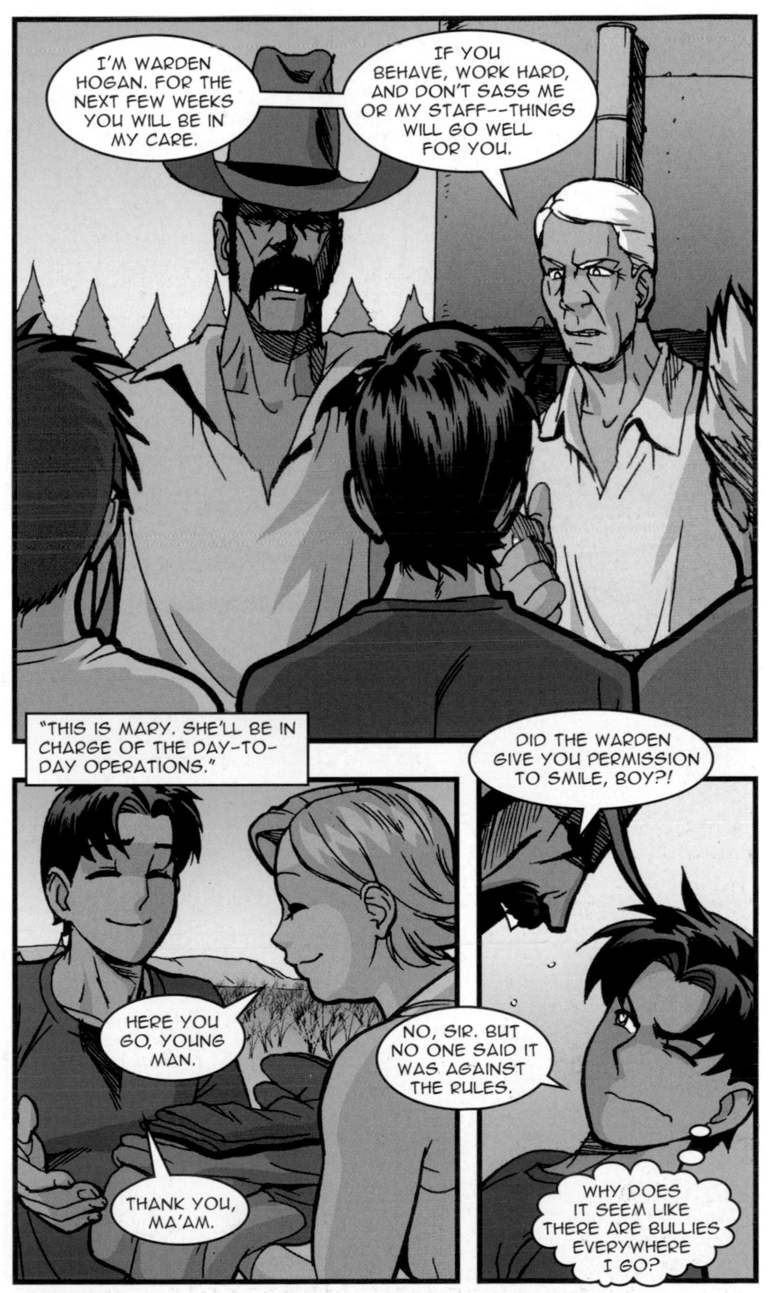
I'M WARDEN HOGAN. FOR THE NEXT FEW WEEKS YOU WILL BE IN MY CARE.
IF YOU BEHAVE, WORK HARD, AND DON'T SASS ME OR MY STAFF--THINGS WILL GO WELL FOR YOU.
"THIS IS MARY. SHE'LL BE IN CHARGE OF THE DAY-TO-DAY OPERATIONS."
HERE YOU GO, YOUNG MAN.
THANK YOU, MA'AM.
DID THE WARDEN GIVE YOU PERMISSION TO SMILE, BOY?!
NO, SIR. BUT NO ONE SAID IT WAS AGAINST THE RULES.
WHY DOES IT SEEM LIKE THERE ARE BULLIES EVERYWHERE I GO?

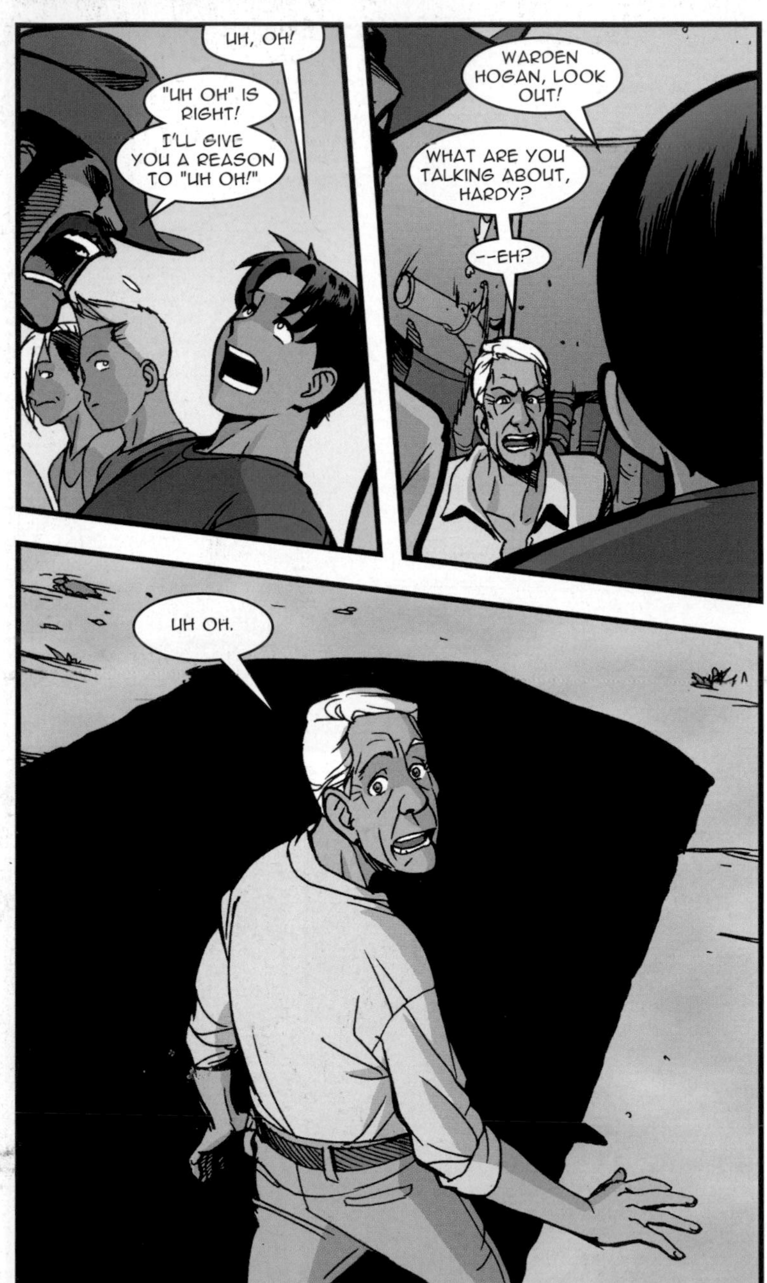
UH, OH!
"UH OH" IS RIGHT!
I'LL GIVE YOU A REASON TO "UH OH!"
WARDEN HOGAN, LOOK OUT!
WHAT ARE YOU TALKING ABOUT, HARDY?
--EH?
UH OH.

CHAPTER FOUR:
"THE WHEAT FROM THE CHAFF!"
GET AWAY!
RUN!
WARDEN?!
NO GOOD! HE'S FROZEN WITH FEAR!

MOM?

YANK!

SKRUNCH!

I'D KEEP MY HEAD DOWN IF I WERE YOU, SIR.
I'M DOWN WITH THAT.
STAND BACK, KIDS!
DID YOU SEE THAT?!
IT WAS, LIKE, AMAZING!

YOU'RE GOING TO BE OKAY, SIR. IT WAS CLOSE BUT--
--EH?!
NO ONE ASKED YOU TO RESCUE ME, KID!
DO YOU EXPECT ME TO CODDLE YOU NOW?!
NO, SIR. NOT AT ALL.

GOOD! BECAUSE NO ONE GETS SPECIAL TREATMENT AROUND HERE!
NOW EVERYONE ELSE--FALL IN!
HMP. IF IT WERE UP TO ME, HE'D BE THE ONE TO FALL IN...
...IN A BIG HOLE.
NOT VERY GRATEFUL.
NOW LET ME INTRODUCE THE NEW CATTLE WRANGLER WE JUST HIRED HERE...

...WE CALL HIM *COWBOY JOE!*
HOWDY, PARDNERS.

THE WARDEN HERE SAID I CAN PICK ANY OF YOU FELLAS OR FILLIES TO BE MY FARM HAND.
THEY CERTAINLY ARE A SORRY LOT OF CITY-SLICKERS. 
TOO FUNNY. JOE IS REALLY ENJOYING HIS UNDERCOVER ROLE.

WELL, PICKIN'S ARE SLIM.
I RECKON I'LL MAKE DUE WITH THE SCRAWNY ONE.
I'LL GIVE YOU SCRAWNY!
WHY, I OUGHT TO--!
ALL RIGHT, ALREADY!
YOU ALL HAVE YOUR CHORES...GET 'ER DONE!

JUST GETTING INTO CHARACTER.

IF YOU NOTICED, THE WORKERS AREN'T VERY NICE TO KIDS HERE.

THEY DON'T SEEM TO TRUST ANYONE.

YEAH, I SEE HIM TOO.

TRY TO KEEP UP, SCRAWNY!
YEHAW!
WHA--?!
OH. GOT IT.
GIDDY UP, THUNDER!
YOU WANTED TO PUT DISTANCE BETWEEN US AND HIM.
AND HAVE FUN DOING IT!
EVEN DANGER IS MORE FUN ON HORSEBACK, NO?

SURE, BUT WE STILL NEED TO FIND OUT WHAT HAPPENED TO THOSE MISSING KIDS.
THEY KEEP SUCH A CLOSE EYE ON EVERYONE--
--I DON'T SEE HOW ANYONE EVEN HAS THE CHANCE TO DISAPPEAR.
I AGREE.
I BET WE BARELY FINISH OUR LUNCH BEFORE JUAN CATCHES UP TO US.

IIIIIIIIIIEEEEEEEEEEEEEEE!
SO MUCH FOR LUNCH.

HELP! SOMEONE-- PLEASE!
I CAN'T SWIM!

CHAPTER FIVE:
"GIDDY UP, UP AND AWAY!"
I RECKON THIS IS A JOB FOR COWBOY JOE.

OR AT LEAST HIS TRUSTY SIDEKICK!
(OH, BROTHER.)
SPLASH!
THE CURRENT HAS GRABBED VIOLET!
THERE'S NOT MUCH CHANCE WE CAN REACH HER!
GLUB!
FORTUNATELY, FRANK--WE HAVE ALTERNATIVES!
A WHIP?!

IT'S MAYBE TEN FEET LONG--SHE'S MUCH FARTHER AWAY THAN THAT!
SNAP!
FOR NOW--TRUE!
KLIK!
BUT THANKS TO THE EGG-HEADS AT A.T.A.C.--

"--NOT VERY FAR AWAY!"
EH?!
IT DIDN'T EVEN HURT!
WISP!
A NANO-PROPELLED BUNGY-WHIP?!
THOSE GUYS THINK OF EVERYTHING!

MY FAVORITE PART IS THE TARGETING DEVICE.
NOT THAT I COULDN'T, YOU KNOW, HAVE DONE IT MYSELF.
NOW BY CONTRACTING THE WHIP, I CAN REEL OUR FRIEND BACK TO SHORE
I'VE GOT IT FROM HERE, JOE.
WE DON'T NEED VIOLET ASKING ABOUT A.T.A.C. TECHNOLOGY.
SO FAR SHE'S BEEN TOO SHAKEN UP TO NOTICE.
RIGHT THIS WAY, VIOLET.
COFF GAK
TH-THANKS

HERE YOU GO--TO KEEP YOU WARM.
GOSH, GUYS...I DON'T KNOW WHAT I WOULD HAVE DONE IF YOU TWO HADN'T COME ALONG.
I'VE ALWAYS BEEN SUCH A BAD GIRL.
NO ONE I'VE EVER KNOWN WOULD HAVE BOTHERED SAVING MY LIFE.
I'M SURE YOU'RE WRONG ABOUT THAT, VIOLET.
CAN YOU TELL US WHAT HAPPENED...? HOW YOU WOUND UP IN THE RIVER?
I CAN TRY, COWBOY JOE...

...BUT THE TRUTH IS I DIDN'T REALLY SEE ANYTHING.

I WAS JUST DOING MY CHORES, SWEEPING THE KITCHEN CABIN.

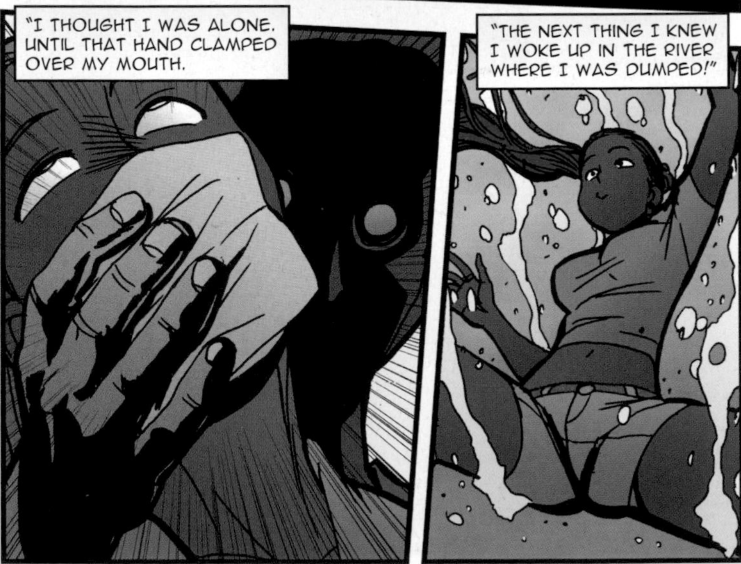

CHLOROFORM?
THE ONLY CHEMICAL THAT COULD HAVE KNOCKED HER OUT SO QUICKLY.

SO, UM--YOU GONNA FIND OUT WHO DID THIS?
OR ARE YOU JUST GOING TO TALK ABOUT IT?
WE'RE GOING TO TRY.
I GUESS HER GRATITUDE HAD A SHORT LIFE.

BUT FIRST, MA'AM, LETS GET YOU HOME SAFELY.
TH-THANK YOU, COWBOY JOE.
MY BROTHER THE CHARMER.

SOON, OUTSIDE THE KITCHEN CABIN...
I DON'T THINK SHE WAS BEING RUDE--SHE JUST NEVER LEARNED ANOTHER WAY.
I HEAR YOU. IT'S KIND OF SAD.

LOCKED. HMM.
THEY MUST KEEP IT LOCKED WHEN NO ONE IS AROUND.
TOGGLE

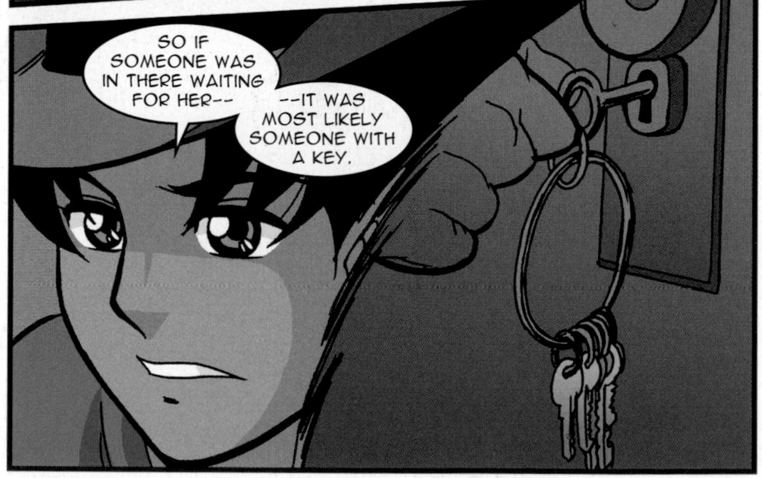
SO IF SOMEONE WAS IN THERE WAITING FOR HER--
--IT WAS MOST LIKELY SOMEONE WITH A KEY.

I SAY WE CHECK ON JUAN THE GUARD FIRST. HE WAS SPYING ON US.
OR WAS THAT ABOUT PRODDING US TOWARDS THE RIVER TO FIND VIOLET?

APPARENTLY HE'S IN CHARGE OF THE BARN TOO.
LET'S START THERE.

HELLO?
MR. BARR? JUAN?
ARE YOU HERE?

HMP. GUESS NOT.

LET'S TRY THE FIELDS.
OKAY. WE SHOULD--
SNF, SNF
FRANK! DO YOU SMELL THAT?!

SMOKE!
SNF, SNF
I DO NOW! IT'S COMING--

--FROM THERE! FROM THE BACK OF THE STABLE!

AND WHERE THERE'S SMOKE, THERE'S--
FWOSH!
YOU REMEMBER!

WE'VE GOT TO GET YOU HORSES OUT OF HERE!
NEIIIGH!

NEIIIGH!
NEIIIGH!
IT'S OKAY, GIRLS--YOU'RE SAFE NOW.

CHAPTER SIX:
"FIRED!"
IT'S JUAN!
HE'S DAZED--
CONFUSED. LIKE
HE'D BEEN HIT ON
THE HEAD!

WE'VE GOT TO REACH HIM BEFORE THE FIRE DOES!
DO YOU HAVE ANY IDEAS...
...FRANK?
WHERE'D HE GO?!
SORRY, I HAD TO PICK UP SOME LAUNDRY.
SO TO SPEAK.
I HEAR YOU...!

I'VE GOT THE OTHER SIDE.
MR. BARR-- WE NEED YOU TO JUMP ONTO THE SHEET!
QUICK THINKING, GENTLEMEN.
LET US HELP.
JUMP, JUAN! THAT'S AN ORDER!
Y-YES, SIR!
IIIIIIIEEEE!

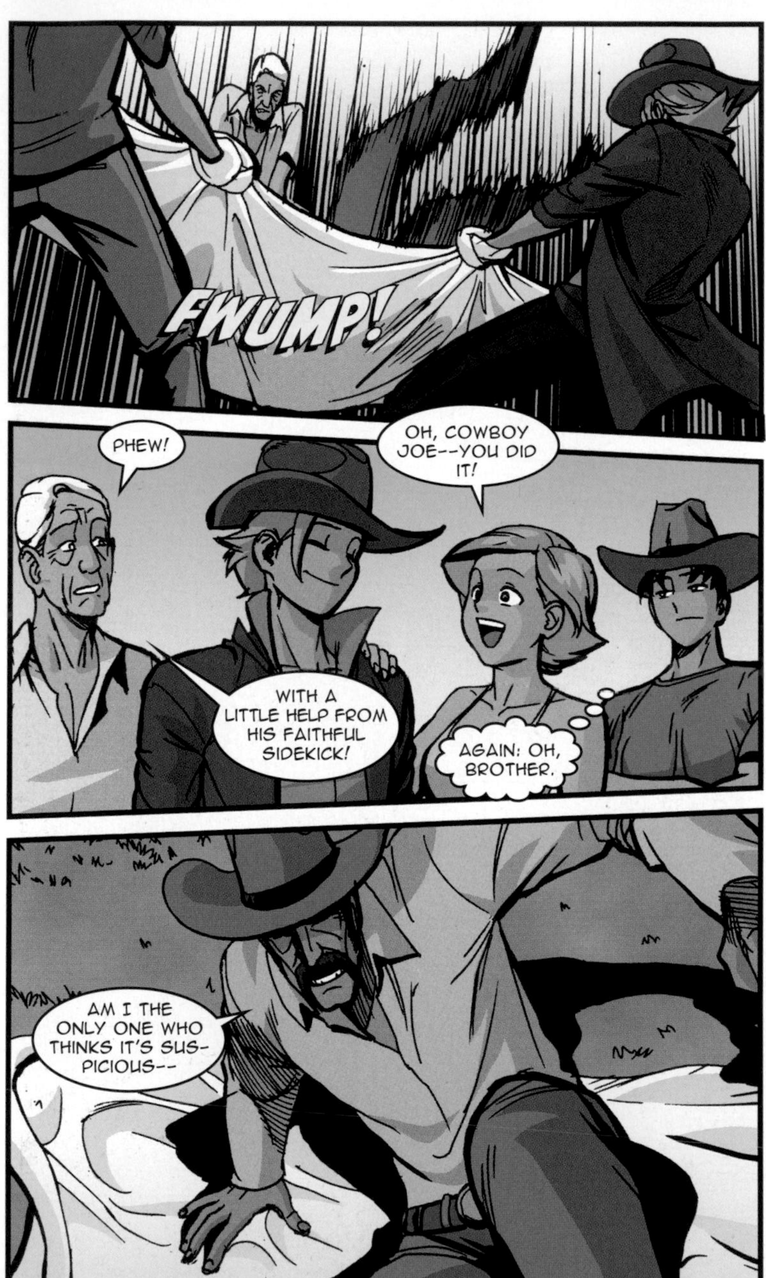
FWUMP!
PHEW!
OH, COWBOY JOE--YOU DID IT!
WITH A LITTLE HELP FROM HIS FAITHFUL SIDEKICK!
AGAIN: OH, BROTHER.
AM I THE ONLY ONE WHO THINKS IT'S SUS-PICIOUS--

--THAT THESE TWO ARE ON HAND WHENEVER THERE'S TROUBLE?!
HOW DO WE KNOW THEY DIDN'T START THE FIRE?!
AND THEN WHAT-- WE RESCUE YOU?!
WHAT WOULD BE THE POINT, SIR?!
JUAN, THEY SAVED YOUR LIFE!
THE FIRE DEPARTMENT IS HERE.
LET'S LET COOLER HEADS PREVAIL.
OF COURSE, SIR. SORRY, SIR.

LATER...

HAVE YOU NOTICED PEOPLE AREN'T BIG ON "THANK YOU'S" AROUND HERE?

REMEMBER, EVEN WITH THE WIDE OPEN SKIES--

--SORROW RANCH IS STILL A DETENTION CENTER.

COULD HE HAVE USED IT TO START THE FIRE IN THE BARN?
I CAN THINK OF ONE WAY TO FIND OUT...

LIGHTS OUT...
ZZZ

ZZZ

ZZZ

...NEITHER ARE CIGARETTES! BUT THAT DOESN'T MEAN I CAN'T TRY TO SNEAK A SMOKE!

A LITTLE LATER...
I HAVE TO TELL YOU, I HATE CASES LIKE THIS.
HOW SO?
WE'RE NO CLOSER TO FINDING THE MISSING KIDS--
--AND ALL THE SUSPECTS HAVE LEAD US NOWHERE.
NOT ALL THE SUSPECTS. THERE'S STILL--
EEEEEEEEEEEEEEEEE!

CHAPTER SEVEN:
"A NOT-SO-
MARVELOUS
BULLPEN!"
IS THIS AS BAD AS IT LOOKS?!
AT LEAST!
EEEEEEEEEEEEE!

WE'VE GOT TO GET IN THERE, NOW!
"IN THERE"?
HONESTLY, I WAS THINKING MORE, LIKE, WE GET HER OUT HERE-- WITH US.
BUT OKAY.
I'M SURE YOU KNOW WHAT YOU'RE DOING.
YOU USUALLY DO.
DON'T WORRY, MA'AM. I'LL GET YOU OUT HERE!
THANK YOU, COWBOY JOE!
WHAT IS YOUR FAITHFUL SIDEKICK DOING?

YE-HAH!
WOO HOO!
MOOO!
?!

LOOK!
THAT'S IT--HE WAS DISTRACTING THE BULL!
I'VE GOT YOU--LET'S GO!
YOUR SIDE-KICK IS VERY FAITHFUL!
IF ONE MORE PERSON CALLS ME A SIDEKICK...
SNORT SNORT!

OF COURSE, THAT'S ONLY IF I PULL THIS OFF!
WHAM!
SORRY, FELLA--
--BUT THIS WAY WE BOTH LIVED!

I HEARD SCREAMS!
DENNIS!
"DENNIS"?
MY BELOVED!
"BELOVED"?
SMEK!
OH, UM... SORRY. GOT A LITTLE CARRIED AWAY--
--IN FRONT OF THE KIDS.
NOTHING TO APOLOGIZE FOR.
TRUE LOVE ROCKS.

YES, IT'S RIGHT UP THERE, OVERLOOKING THE RANCH.
BUT IT'S BEEN ABANDONED FOR YEARS!

NOT MUCH LONGER...
FOR A PATH THAT HASN'T BEEN USED IN A WHILE--
--THERE'S A LOT OF FOOTPRINTS AND TROD MARKS.
GOOD EYE, COWBOY JOE.

SO IF ALL THE SUSPECTS ARE ACCOUNTED FOR--WE KNOW THEY WEREN'T RESPONSIBLE.
AND THEY WERE THE ONLY ONES WHO WERE HERE WHEN THE KIDS DISAPPEARED.

THAT LEAVES THE ONLY PEOPLE WHO KNOW WHERE THE TEENS ARE--
--THE MISSING TEENS THEMSELVES.

CLAP CLAP CLAP CLAP
IS THAT.. APPLAUSE?

CHAPTER EIGHT: "UNHAPPY TRAILS!"
BRAVO! BRAVO!
YOU TWO MUST BE THE SHARPEST PENCILS IN THE BOX.
YOU FIGURED IT ALL OUT.

EVER SINCE WE GOT HERE, WE'VE BEEN TRYING TO THINK OF A WAY TO CLOSE THIS RANCH DOWN!
IF ENOUGH KIDS WENT MISSING THIS PLACE WOULD BE SHUT DOWN.
AND SINCE YOU'RE THE ONLY TWO WHO KNOW WE'RE HERE...
TAP TAP
WRONG.
THIS MIGHT BE THE PERFECT TIME FOR YOU GUYS TO SURRENDER.

LIGHT-- TOO BRIGHT!
CAN'T SEE!
WE DON'T WANT TO SEE ANYONE HURT IF WE CAN AVOID IT.
AND MAYBE YOU CAN ENLIGHTEN US--JUST HOW WAS SHUTTING DOWN THIS RANCH A GOOD IDEA? IT WASN'T PERFECT, BUT IT'S WAY BETTER THAN PRISON.
WE CALLED THE AUTHORITIES AS SOON AS WE REALIZED WHAT YOU KIDS WERE UP TO. WE HAD TO STOP YOU BEFORE ANY MORE LIVES WERE PUT AT RISK IN YOUR INSANE SCHEME.
WHICH SHOULD JUST ABOUT WRAP THINGS UP HERE.

THAT'S WHAT YOU THINK. WE HAD ONE LAST CATASTROPHE PLANNED.
OUR BIGGEST ONE YET!
AND YOU TWO CAN'T STOP IT.
I WOULDN'T BE SO SURE.
GIDDY UP!
"YOU'RE TOO LATE!
"WE PLANTED EXPLOSIVES AT THE CATTLE PEN!
"YOU CAN'T PREVENT--
BLAM!

"...A STAMPEDE!"
RRR

RRRRUMMBL

RRRRUMMBLE!
THOSE TENTS, JUST AHEAD--
--THOSE SLEEPING RANCHERS WILL BE CRUSHED!
TELL ME YOU HAVE SOME LAST MINUTE RES-CUE UP YOUR SLEEVE!
BBBBRRRRUMMMMBBBBLE!

MY SLEEVE?
NOT THIS TIME, NO.
BUT MY BOOT?
OUR BOOTS?
CLIK
NOW THERE'S A LAST MINUTE RESCUE WAITING TO HAPPEN.

THEY'RE LOADED WITH KNOCK-OUT GAS!
I KIND OF WONDERED HOW THEY WERE GOING TO COME IN HANDY.

WHAT THE HECK?!
DENNIS, WHAT'S GOING ON!
WE WERE ALMOST SMUSHED IN OUR SLEEP!
THEY-- THEY SAVED US AGAIN!

CHAPTER NINE:
"INTO THE SUNSET!"
WITH THE BAD ELEMENT GONE FROM THIS PLACE--
--MAYBE WE CAN REALLY MAKE A DIFFERENCE IN THESE KIDS' LIVES.
THERE'S NO DOUBT, SIR.

DO YOU REALLY HAVE TO GO?
I'M AFRAID SO.
I RECKON THERE ARE OTHER PLACES, OTHER PEOPLE THAT NEED OUR HELP.
YOU RECKON THAT, DO YOU?

IF YOU EVER NEED US, WE'RE ONLY A SUNRISE AWAY.
POURING IT ON A BIT THICK, NO?
THEY LOVE THIS COWBOY STUFF.

THOSE WERE TWO VERY BRAVE YOUNG MEN.
AND CUTE, TOO!
I'VE ONLY GOT ONE QUESTION...

...WHO WAS THAT FELLA WITH COWBOY JOE?!
YEEEEE-HAW!
FOR A FINAL TIME: OH, BROTHER.
THE END
MOSEY ALONG NOW, LIL' DOGGIES!

"THE DEADLIEST STUNT"
IIIIIEEEEE!
THEY SAY IN SPACE, NO ONE CAN HEAR YOU SCREAM.
IT'S PRETTY DIFFICULT IN WATER, TOO.
THOUGH NICOLE IS GIVING IT HER BEST SHOT.
CHAPTER ONE: "SCARED HALF TO DEPTH!"

AAAAAAAAAIIIIIIIII

NOT THAT I CAN BLAME HER.
IF I WASN'T SO FOCUSED ON TRYING TO STOP THIS KILLER SHARK FROM EATING US FOR LUNCH--
--I'D BE INCLINED TO DO A LITTLE SHRIEKING MYSELF.
EEEEEEE!

LET'S SEE, THE BEST WAY TO MAKE DO...
...IS TO MAKE DO.
UNCLICK
?!
I'M NOT CARRYING ANY WEAPONS ON ME --
-- SO I'LL HAVE TO IMPROVISE!
RIGHT THIS WAY, MR. TEETH...

WHAM!
...BATTER UP!
I ALMOST FEEL BAD FOR THE GUY.
IT'S NOT HIS FAULT HE'S A NATURAL PREDATOR.
EMPHASIS ON "ALMOST."
NICOLE GOT MY SIGNAL.
THE SOONER WE'RE OUT OF THESE WATERS...THE BETTER!

FWOOSH!
AIR... AT LAST!
YOU DID IT, FRANK! =PANT PANT= YOU SAVED US!
SO FAR. BUT SHARKS ARE NOT USUALLY SO EASILY--
OH, NO!
LOOK!
--DISSUADED.
IT'S COMING BACK!
TELL ME YOU HAVE ANOTHER MIRACLE READY?!
HONESTLY?
FRESH OUT.

SUDDENLY!
SPLOSH!
FRANK--THE SHARK?!
IT LOOKS LIKE HE'S...IN PAIN?
IT-- IT'S LEAVING?
BUT... WHY?
IT SEEMS... FRIGHTENED. BUT...OF WHAT?
THAT WOULD BE ME.
I ALMOST FORGOT YOU WERE ON THE BOAT...
YOU--?! OF COURSE!

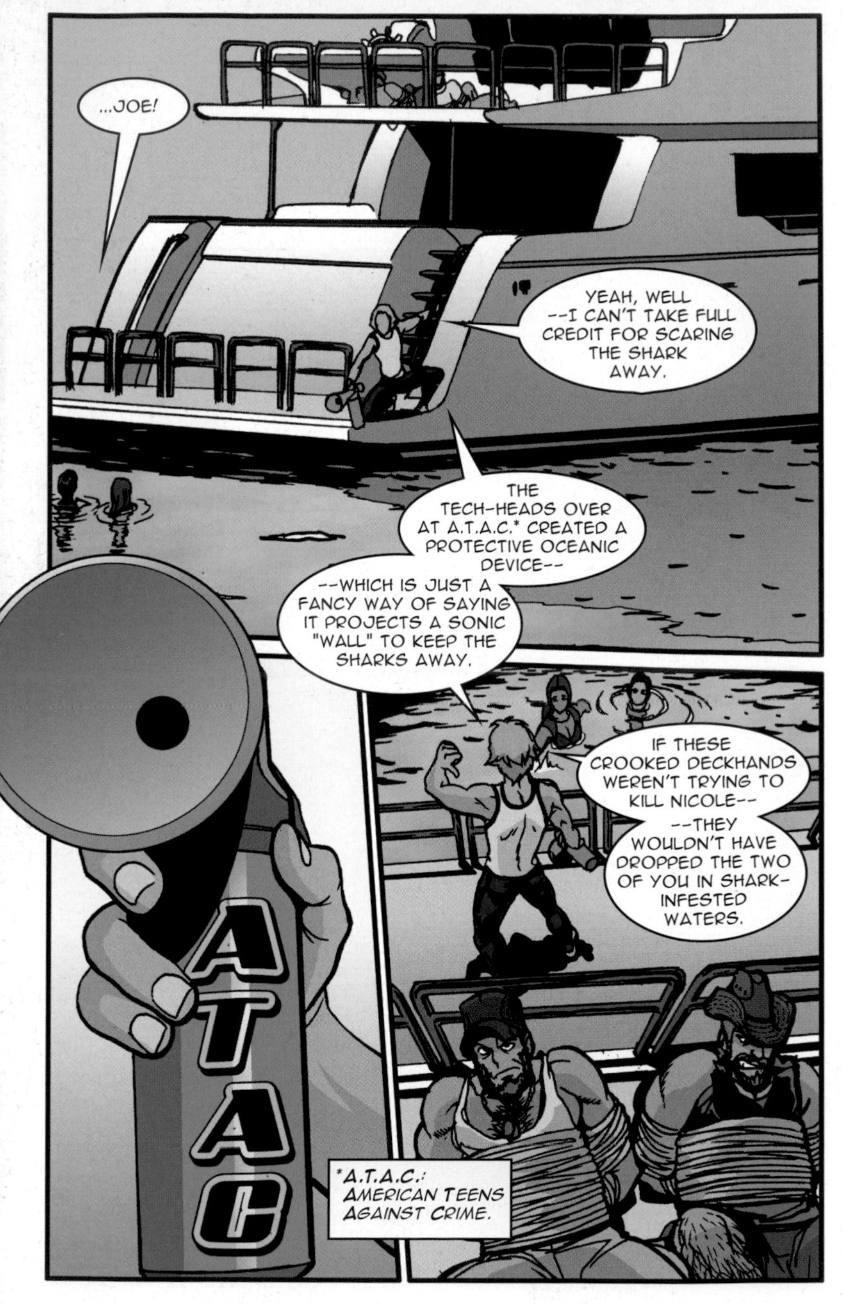
...JOE!
YEAH, WELL --I CAN'T TAKE FULL CREDIT FOR SCARING THE SHARK AWAY.
THE TECH-HEADS OVER AT A.T.A.C.* CREATED A PROTECTIVE OCEANIC DEVICE--
--WHICH IS JUST A FANCY WAY OF SAYING IT PROJECTS A SONIC "WALL" TO KEEP THE SHARKS AWAY.
IF THESE CROOKED DECKHANDS WEREN'T TRYING TO KILL NICOLE--
--THEY WOULDN'T HAVE DROPPED THE TWO OF YOU IN SHARK-INFESTED WATERS.
ATAC
*A.T.A.C.: AMERICAN TEENS AGAINST CRIME.

I OWE YOU BOTH MY LIFE.
WE'RE JUST GLAD WE COULD BREAK UP THIS CHARTER BOAT KIDNAP RING BEFORE ANYONE ELSE WAS HURT.
IT'S ALWAYS AMAZING HOW MANY WAYS PEOPLE TRY TO TAKE ADVANTAGE OF TEENAGERS.
MAYBE EVEN MORE AMAZING--
--IS ALL THE DIFFERENT WAYS WE STOP THEM!

CHAPTER TWO: "CONRAD. BRIAN CONRAD."
THE WORLD HOLDS ITS BREATH. BRIAN CONRAD IS THE WORLD'S MOST FAMOUS SECRET SUPER-AGENT.
DICTATORS SHIVER AT HIS NAME. BAD MEN BEAT A HASTY RETREAT.
WHAT WILL HE DO NEXT?

I CAN HARDLY WAIT TO FIND OUT.
THANKS FOR TELLING US ABOUT THIS, CHET.
SHHHH. THIS IS WHERE IT GETS GOOD!
I AM SURE.

BUT TO DO IT, HE HAS TO JUMP OVER ***THE BARRELS OF DEATH!***
YEAH, SECRET AGENTS TELL PEOPLE WHAT THEY'RE DOING.
NOT HARDLY.

STOP RIGHT THERE, BAD GUY!

YOU'LL NEVER ESCAPE BRIAN CONRAD, SECRET AGENT!

AND HE'S... *AIRBORN!*

WHY DOES HE KEEP REPEATING HIS NAME?
SO HE CAN REMEMBER IT.

FWOOOSH!

UH OH!

THAT WAS BAD.
LIKE NOBODY SAW THAT COMING?
I CAN'T LOOK! IS HE OKAY?
WHOA.
P-BRASHK!
EVERYONE STAY BACK! YOU SHOULD NEVER TRY TO MOVE AN ACCIDENT VICTIM!
WE SHOULD WAIT FOR AN AMBULANCE TO ARRIVE AND LET THE PARAMEDICS CHECK HIM OUT.
STAY STILL, BRIAN. HELP WILL BE HERE SHORTLY.
I'LL CALL 911 ON MY CELL!

LATER...
I KNOW YOU'RE STILL UPSET ABOUT OUR FIGHT,* BUT LISTEN TO THE PARAMEDICS!
I'M TELLING YOU, I'M FINE!
THERE ARE OVER FIVE HUNDRED AND EIGHTY THOUSAND BIKE INJURIES EVERY YEAR.
NEARLY SEVEN HUNDRED OF THOSE ARE DEADLY. WHICH IS WHY YOU SHOULD ALWAYS WEAR A HELMET.
*IN THE PREVIOUS ADVENTURE.
ADMIT IT, FRANK. YOU KIND OF ENJOYED SEE-ING HIM TAKE A SPILL.
NOT AT ALL, JOE. I MIGHT NOT BE BRIAN'S BIGGEST FAN, BUT I DON'T WANT TO SEE ANYONE GET HURT.
LET'S HOPE EVERYONE STAYS SAFE ON OUR NEXT CASE.
THAT "AMBULANCE DRIVER" GAVE ME THIS VIDEO GAME DISC.
LINDSAY RIDER?

CHAPTER THREE:
"[NOT SO] CERTAIN DEATH!"
"SHE GOES BY THE NAME, LINDSAY RIDER!
"SHE DEFIES DEATH!
"ALWAYS WITH A BRILLIANT SMILE ON HER FACE!"
I GUESS THIS IS IT FOR ME, EH?

FWUMP
OR NOT!
YEAH! WOO HOO!
WE LOVE YOU!
GO, LINDSAY!
WHO DOESN'T?
"FIRST AND FOREMOST, SHE IS A PERFORMER!

"SHE IS AMERICA'S TEEN STUNTWOMAN EXTRAORDINAIRE!"
I'LL SAY! SHE'S AWESOME!
RISKING HER LIFE JUST TO ENTERTAIN PEOPLE? SEEMS A LITTLE OVER THE TOP TO ME.
ARE YOU SURE YOU'RE NOT BEING SEXIST, FRANK? YOU AND I RISK OUR LIFE ALL THE TIME.
WE DO IT FOR A.T.A.C. TO HELP OTHER TEENAGERS.
NOW, BE QUIET SO WE CAN LISTEN TO THE REST OF OUR SPECIAL ASSIGNMENT.

"SIMILARLY, IN EUROPE, DANIELLE PINZLOVIA PERFORMS STUNTS FOR MANY TELEVISION SHOWS AND MOVIES.
"SHE TAKES HER WORK VERY SERIOUSLY."
"RED MADDISON IS A YOUNG CANADIAN TEEN WHO IS THAT COUNTRY'S PREMIER STUNTWOMAN.
"DON'T BE DISTRACTED BY HER SMILE. SHE IS A VERY FIERCE COMPETITOR.
"WENDY WEN IS BELOVED THROUGH-OUT ASIA FOR HER TELEVISED STUNTS.
"SHE CONSIDERS HERSELF AN ARTIST. YOU CAN SEE WHY.

"THIS YEAR, ONE OF THE MAJOR STUDIOS IS HOLDING AN INTERNATIONAL COMPETITION.
"THE IDEA IS TO SETTLE THE QUESTION ONCE AND FOR ALL--WHO IS THE WORLD'S MOST TALENTED FEMALE TEEN STUNT PERFORMER.
sonj
"BECAUSE IT IS EXCLUSIVELY FOR YOUNG WOMEN, A.T.A.C. HAS DECIDED THAT IN THIS PARTICULAR CASE--
"--THE TWO OF YOU ARE NOT THE MAIN AGENTS ON THIS ASSIGNMENT.
FIRST INTERNATIONAL COMPETITION FOR FEMALE TEEN STUNT PERFORMERS!
"INSTEAD, YOU TWO ARE SUPPORT STAFF."
WAIT A MINUTE--WE'RE BACK-UP?
APPARENTLY. BUT--WHO ARE WE BACKING UP?

"'LINDSAY RIDER' IS ACTUALLY LINDSAY RAINS.
"HER FLAMBOYANT STAGE PERSONA IS A DISGUISE FOR HER SOBER COMMITMENT TO A.T.A.C."
LOOK AT THAT POUT ON YOUR FACE, JOE.
NOW WHO'S BEING SEXIST?
OH, PLEASE!
IT HAS NOTHING TO DO WITH HER BEING A GIRL.
IT'S JUST... BACK UP? US?
BACK UP?

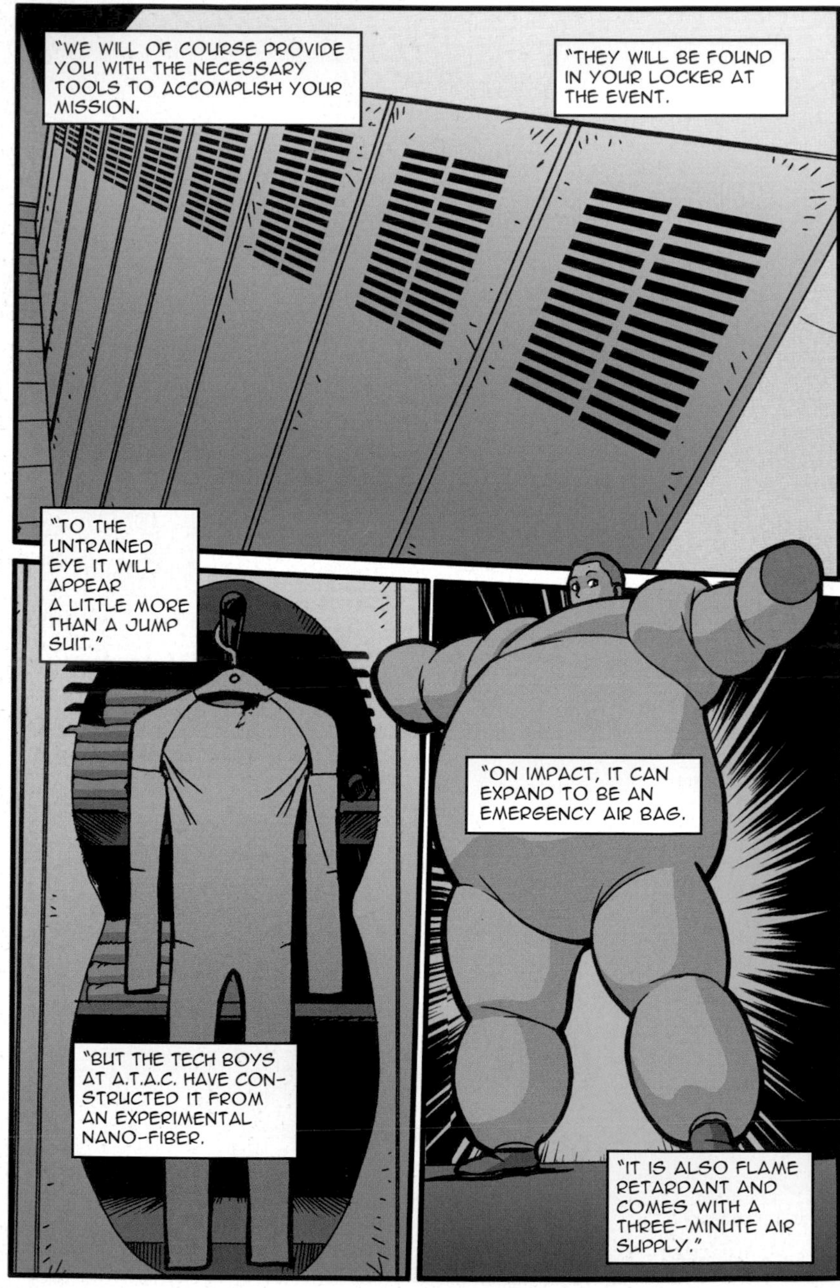
"WE WILL OF COURSE PROVIDE YOU WITH THE NECESSARY TOOLS TO ACCOMPLISH YOUR MISSION.
"THEY WILL BE FOUND IN YOUR LOCKER AT THE EVENT.
"TO THE UNTRAINED EYE IT WILL APPEAR A LITTLE MORE THAN A JUMP SUIT."
"BUT THE TECH BOYS AT A.T.A.C. HAVE CON-STRUCTED IT FROM AN EXPERIMENTAL NANO-FIBER.
"ON IMPACT, IT CAN EXPAND TO BE AN EMERGENCY AIR BAG.
"IT IS ALSO FLAME RETARDANT AND COMES WITH A THREE-MINUTE AIR SUPPLY."

"AS YOU WILL BE FOLLOWING LINDSAY A LOT, WE FELT IT WAS APPROPRIATE FOR HER SUPPORT STAFF TO CARRY A VIDEO CAMERA.
"BE AWARE--
sonj
"THAT THIS CAMERA IS CAPABLE OF PROJECTING HOLOGRAPHIC IMAGES AS WELL, FOR UP TO THIRTY SECONDS.
"THE PROCESS TAKES A LOT OF ENERGY-- AND ALERT!"
VRRRROOOM!
VRRRROOOM!
WHAT THE HECK WAS THAT ABOUT?
I DON'T KNOW--BUT I HAVE A GUESS!

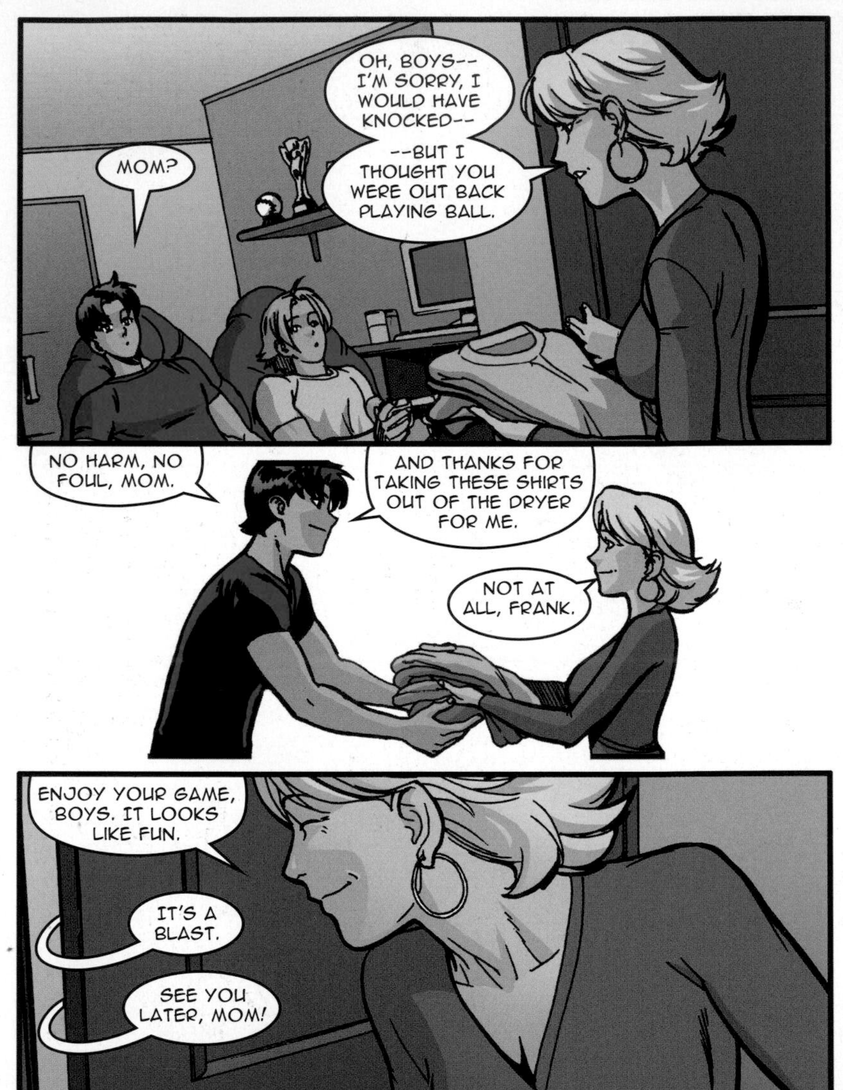
MOM?
OH, BOYS-- I'M SORRY, I WOULD HAVE KNOCKED--
--BUT I THOUGHT YOU WERE OUT BACK PLAYING BALL.
NO HARM, NO FOUL, MOM.
AND THANKS FOR TAKING THESE SHIRTS OUT OF THE DRYER FOR ME.
NOT AT ALL, FRANK.
ENJOY YOUR GAME, BOYS. IT LOOKS LIKE FUN.
IT'S A BLAST.
SEE YOU LATER, MOM!

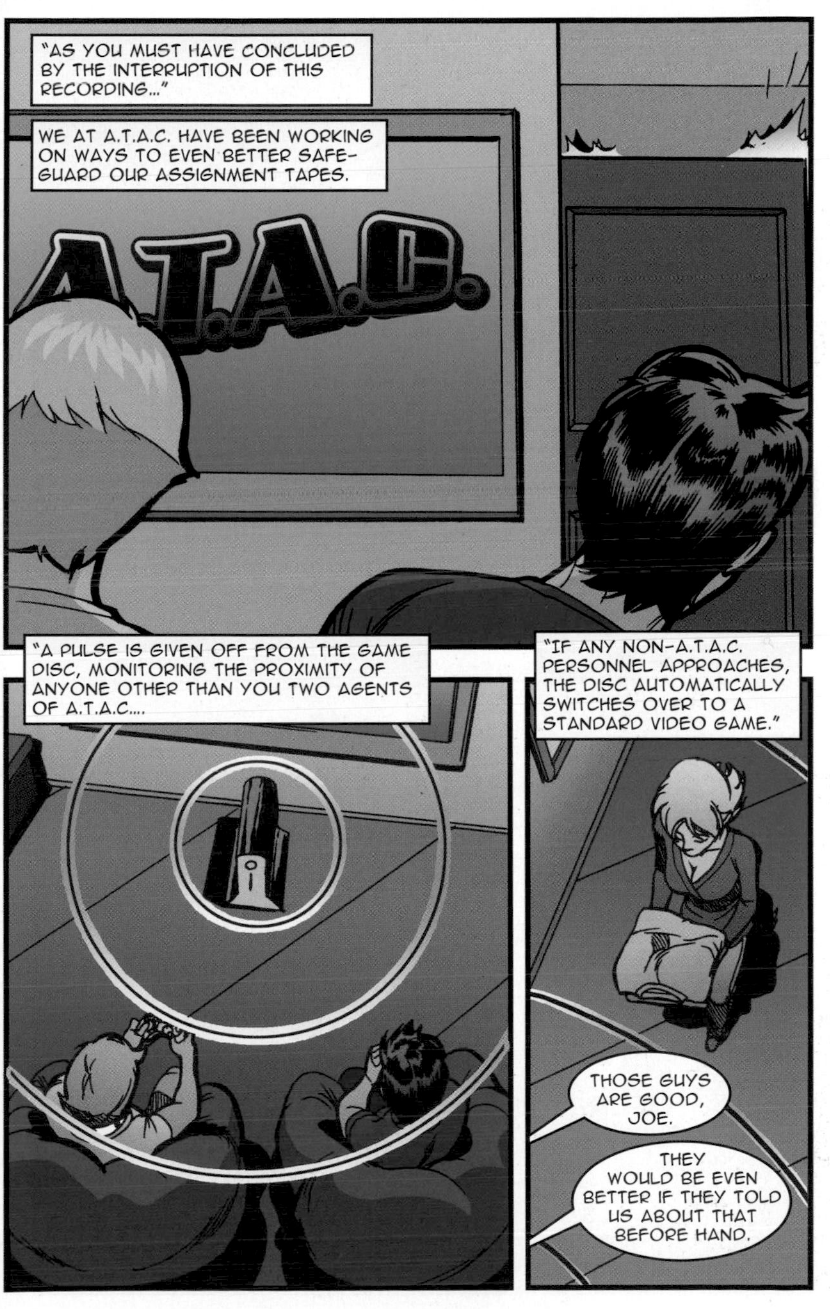
"AS YOU MUST HAVE CONCLUDED BY THE INTERRUPTION OF THIS RECORDING..."
WE AT A.T.A.C. HAVE BEEN WORKING ON WAYS TO EVEN BETTER SAFE-GUARD OUR ASSIGNMENT TAPES.
A.T.A.C.
"A PULSE IS GIVEN OFF FROM THE GAME DISC, MONITORING THE PROXIMITY OF ANYONE OTHER THAN YOU TWO AGENTS OF A.T.A.C....
"IF ANY NON-A.T.A.C. PERSONNEL APPROACHES, THE DISC AUTOMATICALLY SWITCHES OVER TO A STANDARD VIDEO GAME."
THOSE GUYS ARE GOOD, JOE.
THEY WOULD BE EVEN BETTER IF THEY TOLD US ABOUT THAT BEFORE HAND.

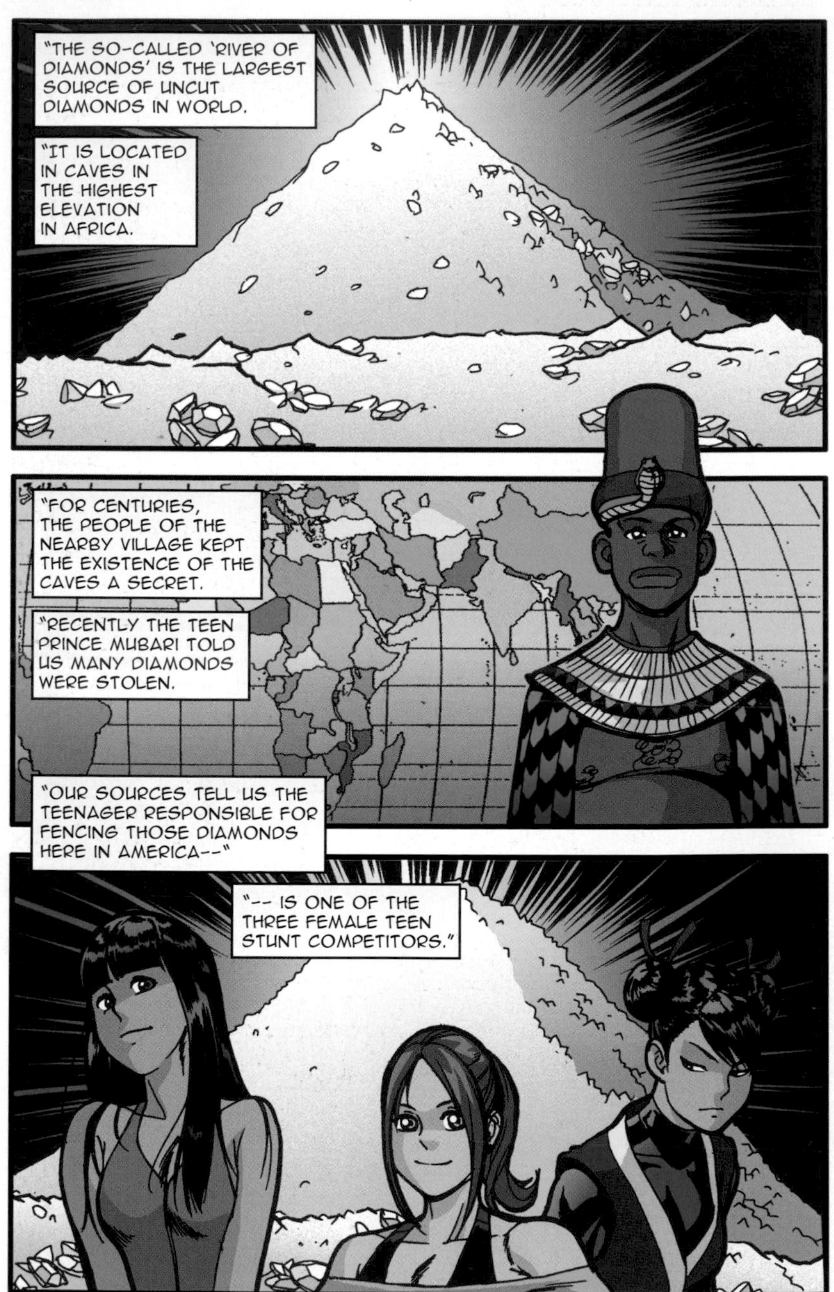
"THE SO-CALLED 'RIVER OF DIAMONDS' IS THE LARGEST SOURCE OF UNCUT DIAMONDS IN WORLD.
"IT IS LOCATED IN CAVES IN THE HIGHEST ELEVATION IN AFRICA.
"FOR CENTURIES, THE PEOPLE OF THE NEARBY VILLAGE KEPT THE EXISTENCE OF THE CAVES A SECRET.
"RECENTLY THE TEEN PRINCE MUBARI TOLD US MANY DIAMONDS WERE STOLEN.
"OUR SOURCES TELL US THE TEENAGER RESPONSIBLE FOR FENCING THOSE DIAMONDS HERE IN AMERICA--"
"-- IS ONE OF THE THREE FEMALE TEEN STUNT COMPETITORS."

"UNFORTUNATELY, SHE'LL USE THE COVER OF THIS YOUNG PERSONS EVENT TO COMMIT HER CRIME--
"--THEREBY PUTTING MANY INNOCENT TEENS AT RISK.
"GOOD LUCK, GENTLEMEN."
BACK-UP?
IT'S AN ALL-GIRL COMPETITION, JOE. STOP TAKING IT SO HARD.
AREN'T THERE FEMALE A.T.A.C. AGENTS THAT CAN BACK HER UP FOR SOMETHING LIKE THIS?
LET IT GO, JOE.
BRRRMMMMM!

CHAPTER FOUR:
"THE END BEGINS!"
LADIES AND GENTLEMEN...
...OR SHOULD I JUST SAY "BOYS AND GIRLS"? BECAUSE TODAY'S EVENT DRAWS ON A YOUNG AUDIENCE FROM ALL OVER THE WORLD!
I'M JEREMY HAFTEL,THE WORLD'S YOUNGEST T.V. HOST, WE ARE HERE TO CELEBRATE FOUR VERY BRAVE AND TALENTED TEEN STUNTWOMEN!

"THE MAJOR FILM STUDIO THAT IS SPONSORING THIS EVENT--
"-- HAS CREATED AN ALIEN LANDSCAPE TO BEST TEST OUR CONTESTANTS!

"BUT DON'T BE FRIGHTENED! IT ONLY LOOKS LIKE A RIVER OF MOLTEN LAVA!

"CERTAINLY, THIS RUGGED TERRAIN WILL FORCE THESE YOUNG LADIES TO FOCUS AND BRING THEIR A GAME!

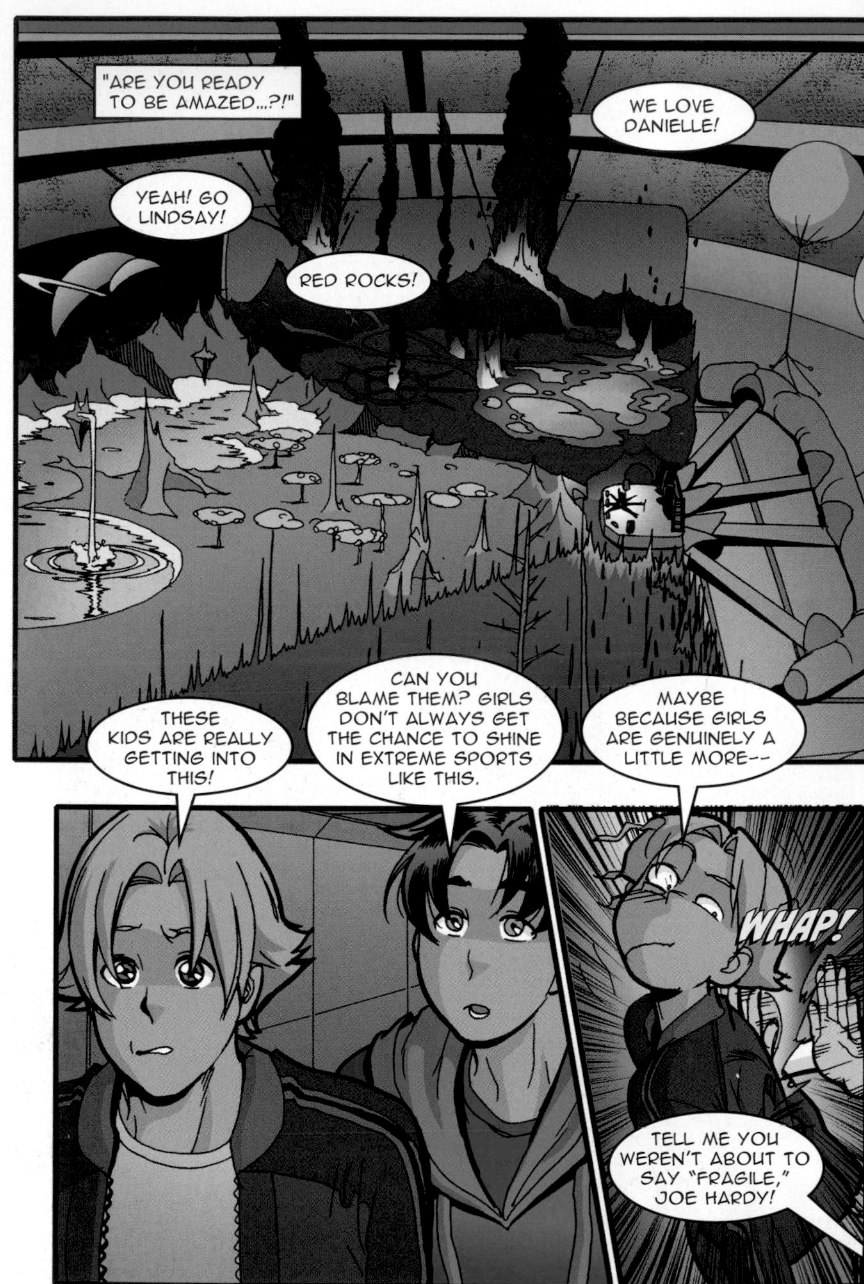
"ARE YOU READY TO BE AMAZED...?!"
WE LOVE DANIELLE!
YEAH! GO LINDSAY!
RED ROCKS!
THESE KIDS ARE REALLY GETTING INTO THIS!
CAN YOU BLAME THEM? GIRLS DON'T ALWAYS GET THE CHANCE TO SHINE IN EXTREME SPORTS LIKE THIS.
MAYBE BECAUSE GIRLS ARE GENUINELY A LITTLE MORE--
WHAP!
TELL ME YOU WEREN'T ABOUT TO SAY "FRAGILE," JOE HARDY!

HOWDY, BOYS.
I'M LINDSAY, BUT WHO DOESN'T KNOW THAT?
HEE HEE
AND I'M FRANK. IF THERE'S ANYTHING WE CAN DO FOR YOU--
IF I THINK OF ANYTHING, I'M SURE YOU'LL BE THE FIRST PERSON I CALL.
LET ME SHOW YOU TO THE LOCKER ROOM.
JOE, BE A DEAR AND BRING MY DUFFEL BAG?
NO PROBLEM.
UNGH!
--LINDSAY.
YES, I WAS GOING TO SAY 'FRAGILE.'

TA DA!
YOU CERTAINLY KNOW HOW TO MAKE AN ENTRANCE.
YOU SHOULD SEE MY EXIT!
TEE HEE!
WHAT DO YOU HAVE IN THIS BAG--
URG
--BRICKS?
OKAY, GUYS A.T.A.C. AGENT TO A.T.A.C. AGENT:
I MAKE IT ALL LOOK EASY, I'M SURE, BUT THIS IS A VERY DANGER-OUS CASE.

DANIELLE SPENDS HER FREE TIME AWAY FROM THE REST OF THE GROUP.

SHE'S A BIG NATURE FAN.

AND RED? SHE'S LIKE THE ULTIMATE TOURIST.

SHE JUST LOVES EXPLORING EVERYTHING ABOUT OUR COUNTRY WHILE SHE'S HERE.

AH, THERE YOU ARE!
EH?
?!

TA TA, BOYS! I'LL SEE YOU AT DINNER!
I'LL GIVE HIM "WORKER BEES."
WHAT ARE WE SUPPOSED TO DO NOW?
GO POLISH HER MOTOR-CYCLE OR SOME-THING EQUALLY DEGRADING?
JOE, WE'RE UNDERCOVER SUPPORT.
WHERE IS IT WRITTEN WE HAVE TO BE CENTER STAGE FOR EVERY CASE?
NOW QUIT YOUR GROUSING AND GET DRESSED.
GREAT. NOT TOO EM-BARRASSING.

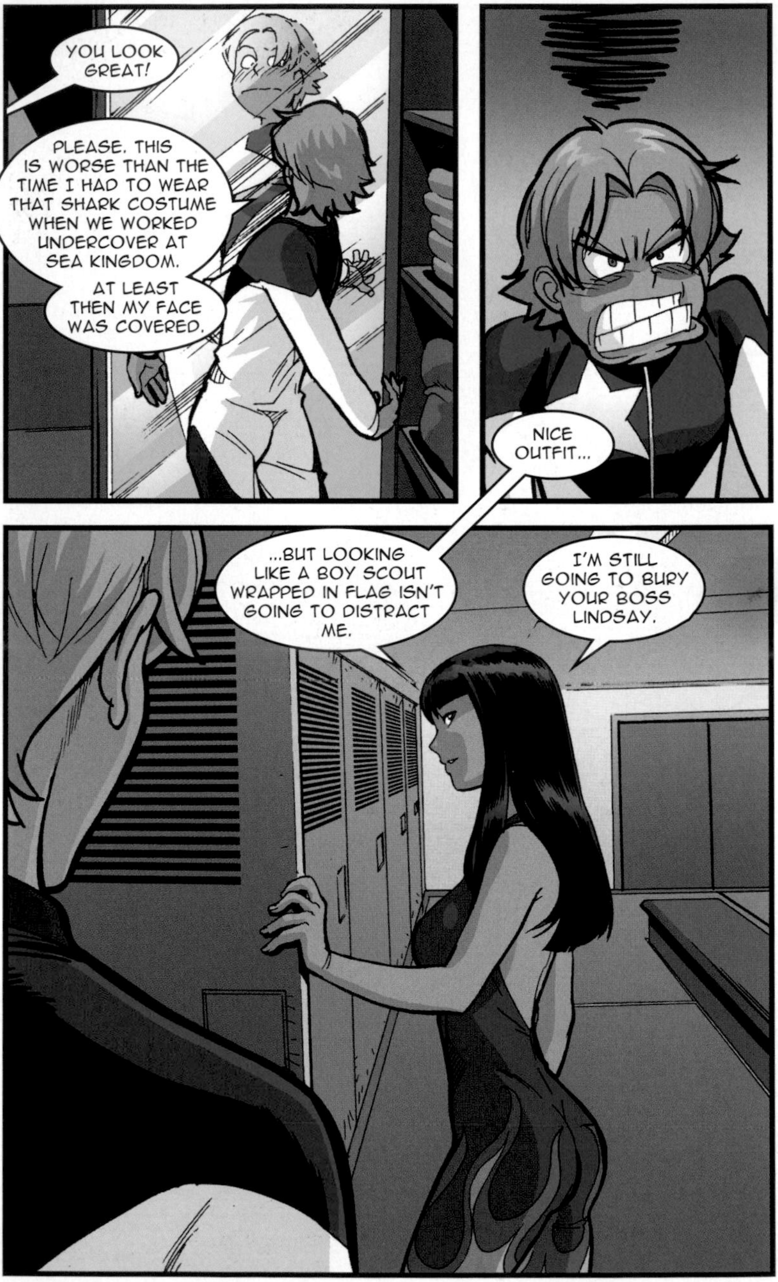

...BUT LOOKING LIKE A BOY SCOUT WRAPPED IN FLAG ISN'T GOING TO DISTRACT ME.

I'M STILL GOING TO BURY YOUR BOSS LINDSAY.

NOT MUCH LATER...
...AT THE CELEBRATORY DINNER AT A NEARBY RESTAURANT...
SAY HEY, CUTEY BOY. IS THIS SEAT TAKEN?
NO, FEEL FREE.
AND TECHNICALLY IT IS "HARDY BOY." BUT THAT SOUNDS SILLY WHEN I SAY IT OUT LOUD.
HEE HEE.

EXCUSE ME...
EH?
POK!
...THAT'S MY CHAIR!

WHAM!
URGN!

LET ME GO! WHAT DO YOU THINK YOU ARE DOING?!

I'M ENDING THIS FIGHT RIGHT HERE AND NOW!

FIGHTING? ME?

HEE HEE.

NEVER. I'M A LADY, AFTER ALL.

I WONDER WHERE DANIELLE IS.

CLAP CLAP

I WAS JUST THINKING THE SAME THING.

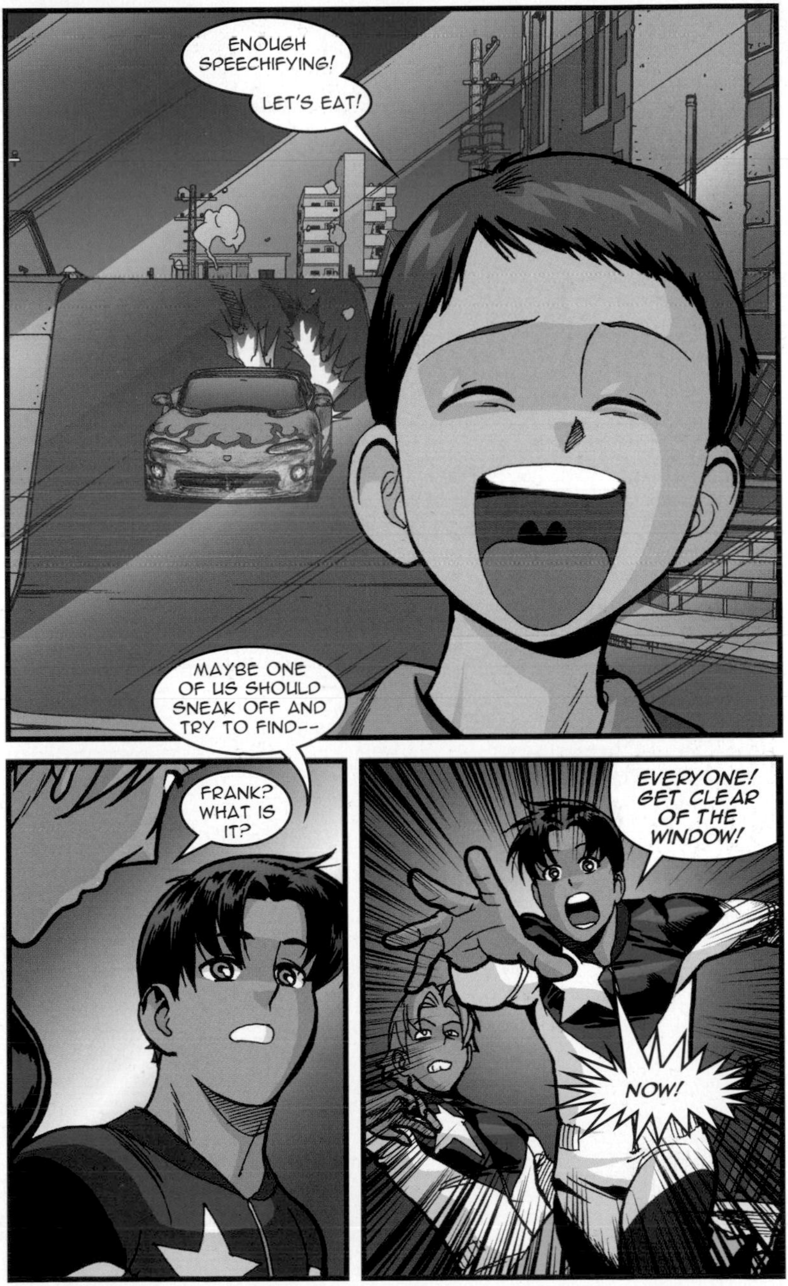

ENOUGH SPEECHIFYING!
LET'S EAT!
MAYBE ONE OF US SHOULD SNEAK OFF AND TRY TO FIND--

CHAPTER FIVE:
"SCREEEECH!"
KRASH!
ONE MOMENT IT IS A SIMPLE DINNER PARTY. THE NEXT...?
PANDEMONIUM!

JEREMY IS RIGHT BY THE WINDOW!
I HAVE TO GET HIM OUT OF THE WAY BEFORE IT IS--
TOO LATE, FRANK!
I'VE GOT HIM!
WUMP!
THANKS, LINDSAY--
--BUT WHO'S GOING TO SAVE FRANK?!
SCREEECH!

HUNH?!

BETTER TO LEAVE THE STUNTS TO US PROFESSIONALS, YOUNG MAN?
"YOUNG MAN"? WE'RE THE SAME AGE.
OH, AND THANKS.

THAT WAS CLOSE!
MAYBE NOT AS CLOSE AS YOU THINK.
HEE HEE

THANK YOU! THANK YOU!
KEEP APPLAUDING, BUT THANK YOU.
CONGRATULATIONS, EVERYONE!
YOUR TIMING WAS PERFECT!
STUNTS ROCK!
CLAP CLAP CLAP CLAP

THEY PLANNED ALL THIS?
ON PURPOSE?
FOR FUN?
APPARENTLY.

I THOUGHT SECRET AGENTS TOOK CHANCES.
STUNT PEOPLE ARE A STRANGE BREED, HUH?
CLAP CLAP
THIS ONLY MAKES OUR JOB THAT MUCH HARDER.

A LITTLE LATER...
... BACK AT THE STUDIO-PROVIDED STUNT COURSE...
"WHILE EVERYONE HAS GONE TO BED -- "
--WE SHOULD MAKE OURSELVES FAMILIAR WITH THIS PLACE.
IT'S BOUND TO BE THE SCENE OF THE CRIME...
EVENTUALLY.
I WAS JUST THINKING THE SAME THING.
OH. WHAT WAS THAT?

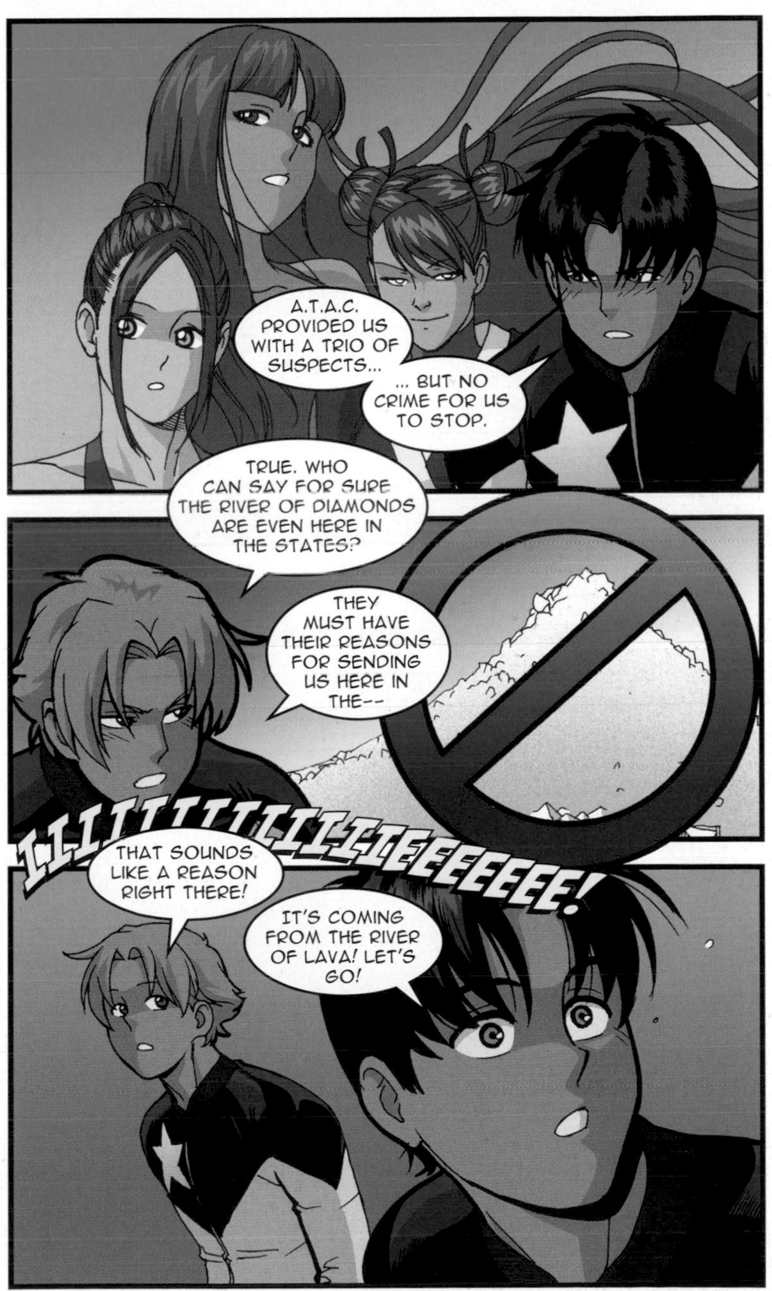
A.T.A.C. PROVIDED US WITH A TRIO OF SUSPECTS...
... BUT NO CRIME FOR US TO STOP.
TRUE. WHO CAN SAY FOR SURE THE RIVER OF DIAMONDS ARE EVEN HERE IN THE STATES?
THEY MUST HAVE THEIR REASONS FOR SENDING US HERE IN THE--
IIIIIIIIIIIIIIEEEEEEEE!
THAT SOUNDS LIKE A REASON RIGHT THERE!
IT'S COMING FROM THE RIVER OF LAVA! LET'S GO!

IIIIIIIIIIIIIEEEEEEEEE!

IT SOUNDS LIKE ONE OF THE GIRLS!

WE'LL KNOW SOON ENOUGH.

CHAPTER SIX:
MOLTEN LAVA, MOLTEN LAVA, EVERYWHERE AND NOT A DROP TO DRINK!"
HELP! SOMEBODY! HELP ME!
RED?!

NOT TO CAST ASPERSIONS, BUT--
ARE YOU REALLY IN TROUBLE OR IS THIS ANOTHER SET-UP?
WHAT KIND OF QUESTION IS THAT?!
OF COURSE IT'S REAL! IT'S ALL REAL!
NOW HELP ME ALREADY!
OKAY, WE HAD TO ASK-- RIGHT?
WAIT A MOMENT, JOE. YOU CAN'T JUST DIVE IN WITHOUT A PLAN.

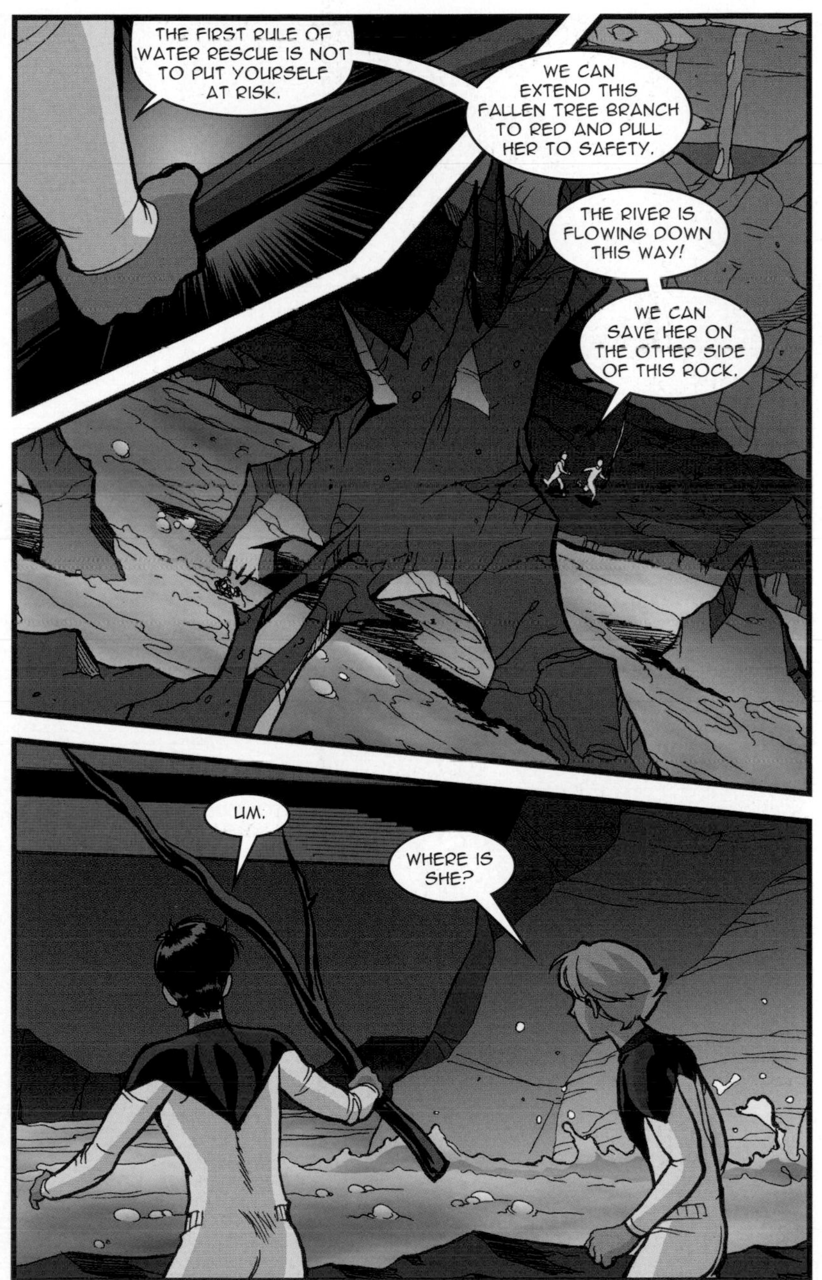
THE FIRST RULE OF WATER RESCUE IS NOT TO PUT YOURSELF AT RISK.
WE CAN EXTEND THIS FALLEN TREE BRANCH TO RED AND PULL HER TO SAFETY.
THE RIVER IS FLOWING DOWN THIS WAY!
WE CAN SAVE HER ON THE OTHER SIDE OF THIS ROCK.
UM.
WHERE IS SHE?

RED?! ARE YOU--?
OH.
WHY DO I FEEL WE SHOULD HAVE KNOWN BETTER THIS TIME?
RELAX, GUYS. THE GIRLS HAVE EVERYTHING UNDER CONTROL!
BUT YOU HAVE TO ADMIT, LINDSAY--
--THEY'RE AWFULLY CUTE WHEN THEY DO THAT RESCUE THANG.
HEE HEE

ONE CAMPFIRE LATER...
SO... EVEN THOUGH YOU INSISTED YOU REALLY WERE IN DANGER--
--YOU WERE JUST PRACTICING FOR THE DUEL STUNT PART OF TOMOR-ROW'S EVENT?

IF WE DON'T HAVE AUTHENTICITY, WE HAVE NOTHING.
BUT I GUESS I'M SORRY IF WE SCARED YOU.
G'NIGHT, EVERYONE. I HAVE TO BE UP EARLY TOMORROW.

"SCARED"? I DIDN'T SAY I WAS SCARED.

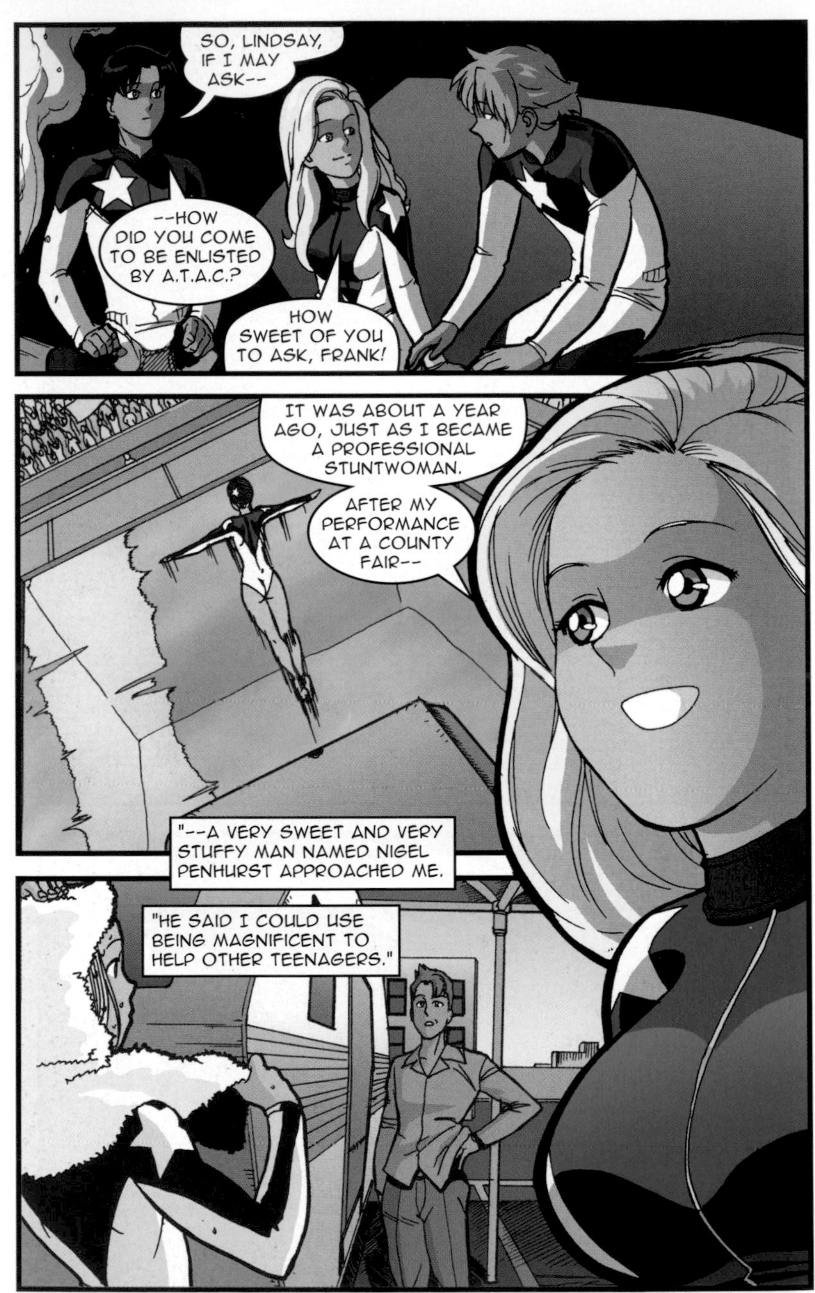
SO, LINDSAY, IF I MAY ASK--
--HOW DID YOU COME TO BE ENLISTED BY A.T.A.C.?
HOW SWEET OF YOU TO ASK, FRANK!
IT WAS ABOUT A YEAR AGO, JUST AS I BECAME A PROFESSIONAL STUNTWOMAN.
AFTER MY PERFORMANCE AT A COUNTY FAIR--
"--A VERY SWEET AND VERY STUFFY MAN NAMED NIGEL PENHURST APPROACHED ME.
"HE SAID I COULD USE BEING MAGNIFICENT TO HELP OTHER TEENAGERS."

I'VE BEEN ON MANY ASSIGN-MENTS SINCE THEN. ALONE.
AND JUST TO BE CLEAR, I DIDN'T ASK FOR HELP THIS TIME AROUND.
I THINK IT WOULD BE BETTER FOR EVERY-ONE INVOLVED IF YOU JUST STAYED OUT OF MY WAY.
NO OFFENSE, GUYS.

I HOPE WE DON'T ACT LIKE THAT WHEN WE HAVE BACK-UP AGENTS SUPPORTING US.
NEVER. BUT SHE MAY HAVE A POINT.
MAYBE WE'VE EXAMINED THIS CASE ALL WRONG.
THERE'S A VERY FAMOUS PLAY BY TOM STOPPARD CALLED "ROSENCRANTZ AND GUILDENSTERN ARE DEAD."
IT'S ABOUT TWO MINOR CHARACTERS IN HAMLET, A PLAY BY SHAKESPEARE.
MAYBE WE'RE JUST HAVING A HARD TIME ADJUSTING TO THE FACT WE'RE HERE TO SUPPORT ANOTHER AGENT.
WE'RE NOT HERE TO SOLVE THIS PARTICULAR CASE.

SO I'M ROSENCRANTZ AND YOU'RE GUILDENSTERN?
YOU COULD LOOK AT IT THAT WAY.

HMMM.
WHAT ARE YOU LOOKING AT?

A HIDDEN DOOR.
CREEEEAK

WHAT HAPPENED TO THIS NOT BEING ABOUT US?
I COULD BE RIGHT.
BUT LET'S CHECK IT OUT ANYWAY. IN CASE I'M WRONG.
ANY ONE OF THE SUSPECTS COULD TAKE THE DIAMONDS DOWN HERE AND HAND THEM OFF TO A FENCE.
TRUE.
OR THEY COULD BE DOWN HERE ALREADY.
OR...

CHAPTER SEVEN: "CLIFFLESS HANGER!"

...THIS COULD JUST BE A REALLY BIG MAINTENANCE ROOM.

WITH PIPES AND PUMPS AND WHATNOT.

SOMETHING HAS TO GENERATE THAT FAKE RIVER UP THERE--THAT'S FOR SURE.

THERE'S NOTHING STORED BENEATH THE GENERATORS.
JUDGING FROM THIS DUST, NO ONE HAS BEEN DOWN HERE FOR A FEW DAYS.
SAME THING UP HERE.
IF THE DIAMOND SMUGGLER CAME THROUGH HERE, SHE DIDN'T LEAVE A TRACE.
I'M STUMPED. ANY IDEAS?
JUST ONE, ACTUALLY.

LATER...
ARE YOU SERIOUS, FRANK?
WE'RE JUST SUPPOSED TO GO TO BED?
KLIK
A.T.A.C. MADE US BACK-UP ON THIS CASE FOR A REASON, JOE.
LINDSAY WILL CALL US IF SHE NEEDS US.
GOOD NIGHT.
I HATE THIS CASE.

WOW. IT NEVER CEASES TO AMAZE ME--

--HOW EVERYTHING FROM BASEBALL CARDS, TO SCI FI, TO PRO WRESTLING, TO NASCAR --

--ALL HAVE THEIR OWN RABID FAN BASES.

AND NOW TEEN STUNT GIRLS.

WHO KNEW?

IN A BIT...

OKAY, I OFFICIALLY DECLARE LINDSAY'S CAR PREPARED FOR VICTORY.

WAIT...!

I'VE GOT TO RECORD YOUR DECLARATION FOR POSTERITY.

THANKS, FRANK. FOR GETTING WITH THE PROGRAM.
WE'RE ALL PART OF THE SAME TEAM.
IT'S TAKEN SOME ADJUSTING IN THE WAY WE WOULD DEAL WITH A CASE.
BUT IF A.T.A.C. LIKES YOU...
WHAT'S NOT TO LIKE?
I CAN'T THINK OF A THING.
GOOD LUCK!

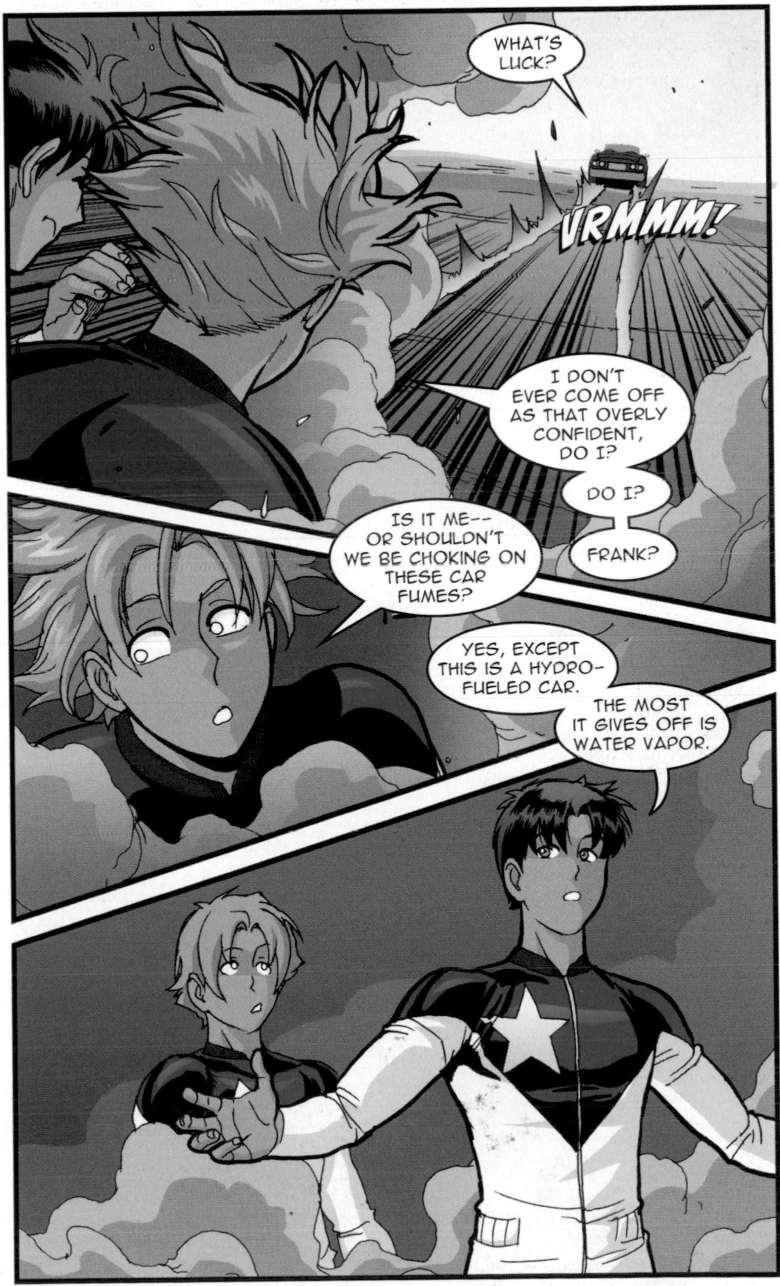
WHAT'S LUCK?
VRMMM!
I DON'T EVER COME OFF AS THAT OVERLY CONFIDENT, DO I?
DO I?
FRANK?
IS IT ME-- OR SHOULDN'T WE BE CHOKING ON THESE CAR FUMES?
YES, EXCEPT THIS IS A HYDRO-FUELED CAR.
THE MOST IT GIVES OFF IS WATER VAPOR.

AND THE RACE IS ON--WITH ALL FOUR GIRLS ANGLING TO BE THE FIRST ONE OVER THE RAMP!
TO THE SURPRISE OF ALMOST NO ONE AT ALL --
--IT'S LINDSAY! AND THE CROWD GOES WILD!

I COULDN'T HAVE DONE IT WITHOUT THE FANS!
IT'S OFFICIAL. I'M MOSTLY IN LOVE.
YOU AND EVERYONE ELSE IN THE STADIUM.
WAIT A MINUTE! WHAT IS GOING ON?!
DOWN THERE ON THE TRACK...

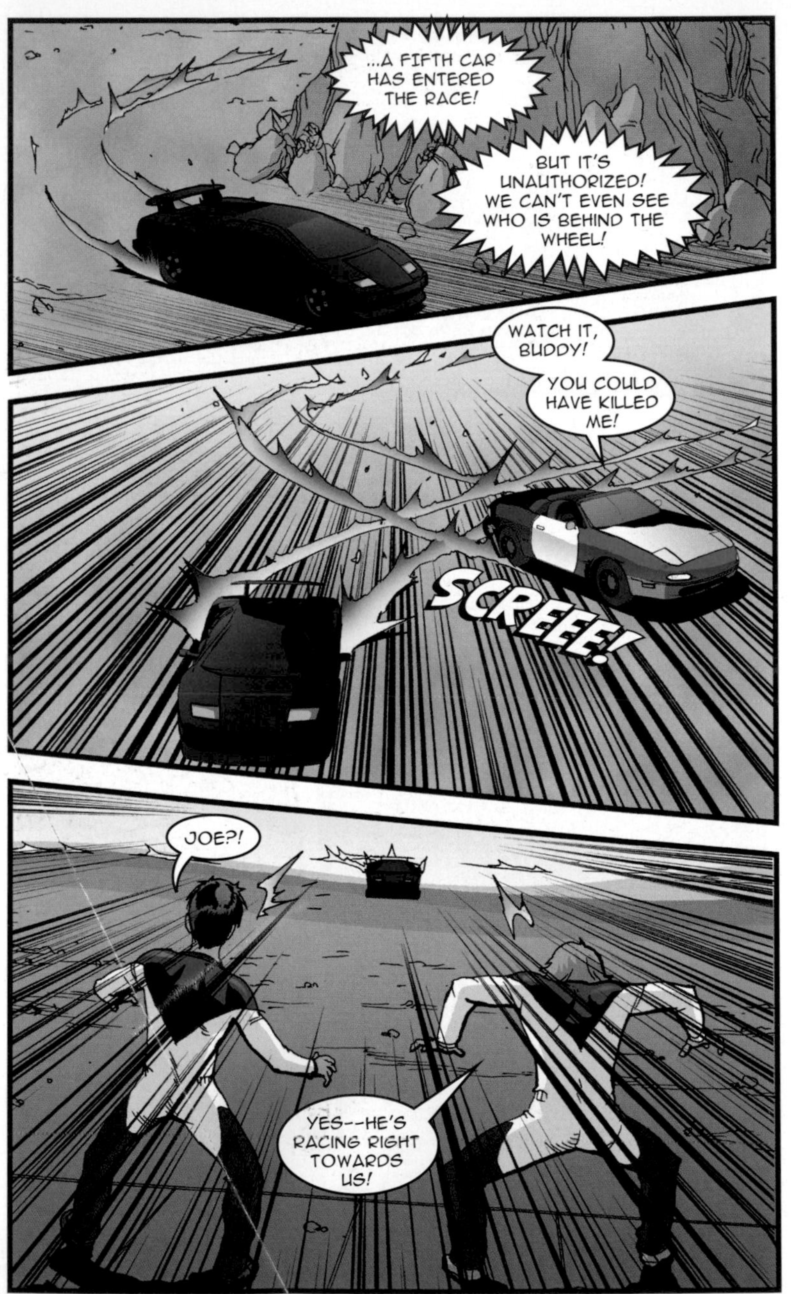
...A FIFTH CAR HAS ENTERED THE RACE!
BUT IT'S UNAUTHORIZED! WE CAN'T EVEN SEE WHO IS BEHIND THE WHEEL!
WATCH IT, BUDDY!
YOU COULD HAVE KILLED ME!
SCREEE!
JOE?!
YES--HE'S RACING RIGHT TOWARDS US!

HEAD FOR THE UTILITY GARAGE!
DO YOU REALLY THINK THAT'S GOING TO SAVE US?
NOPE.
BARABRAOOM!

CREAK!

FRANK, LOOK-- THERE WAS NO DRIVER?
THE CAR MUST HAVE BEEN REMOTE CON- TROLLED.

LET'S GET OUT OF HERE NOW. THESE NANOTECH SUITS ARE ONLY GOOD FOR A SHORT TIME.

HOW ARE WE SUPPOSED TO EXPLAIN HOW WE SURVIVED THAT BLAST?
WE DON'T.

THEY'LL JUST THINK IT WAS PART OF THE SHOW.
CRAZY.
AMAZING!
AWESOME!
YOWZA!

THIS IS UNFAIR!
THEY'RE NOT EVEN PART OF THE COMPETITION!
WHAT CAN I SAY, GIRLS?

FRANK--WHERE DID LINDSAY GO?

HER CAR IS OVER THERE BUT SHE'S NOWHERE TO BE FOUND.

WE WOULD HAVE SPOTTED HER HEADING TO HER TRAILER.

WHICH MEANS SHE MUST HAVE ENTERED THE FAUX JUNGLE.

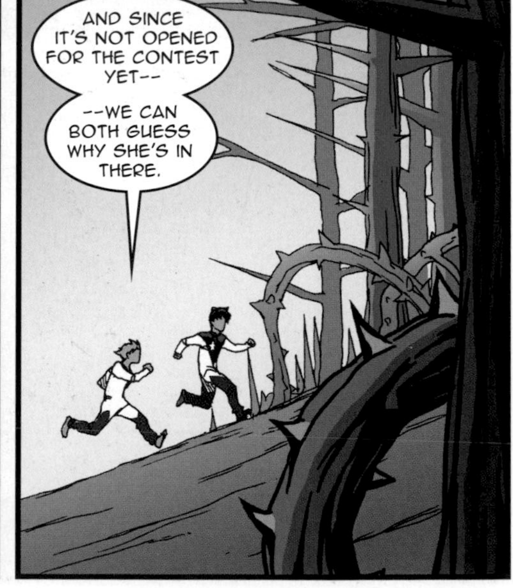

DID YOU ALSO NOTICE RED WASN'T ON THE PODIUM?
YOU'RE SAYING SHE'S THE DIAMOND SMUGGLER?
HONESTLY? I DON'T THINK SHE IS BRIGHT ENOUGH TO--
SHHHH.
HEAR THAT?
A VERY HEATED CON-VERSATION--
--COMING FROM THE OTHER SIDE OF THE WATERFALL?

YOU GAVE YOURSELF AWAY WHEN YOU USED THE RADIO CONTROLLED CAR AS A DISTRACTION.

YOU NEEDED A CLEAR LINE OF SITE IN ORDER TO MANIPULATE.

YOU FIGURED OUT I DID IT FROM IN HERE.

BUT I GUESS YOU DIDN'T HAVE TIME TO ALERT YOUR FELLOW AGENTS OR THEY WOULD HAVE SNEAKED UP ON ME.

CLICK

HEY, LINDSAY.

GUYS.

GUYS, THIS IS THOMAS WALDSWORTH. HE IS A FENCE OF WORLD RENOWN.

A.T.A.C. LEAKED THE INFORMATION ABOUT YOU TWO BECAUSE THEY KNEW HE'D FLUSH HIMSELF OUT BY ATTACKING YOU.

I'VE BEEN SMUGGLING CONTRABAND THROUGH THESE TEEN EVENTS FOR MONTHS NOW.

THIS WAS SUPPOSED TO BE MY FINAL, BIG SCORE.

I'M SURE YOU'LL UNDERSTAND WHY I DON'T WANT ANY WITNESSES?

CH-KLIK!

BIG STICKS, THOUGH?
PERFECTLY ACCEPTABLE!

BEFORE WE TAKE YOU DOWN, WADSWORTH?
GO TEAM LINDSAY!
YOU'RE TEASING, RIGHT?
GET OUT OF HERE, KID, BEFORE--
UHN?!

MOSTLY.
MR. WADSWORTH. YOU HAVE THE RIGHT TO REMAIN SILENT...

OVER HERE, JOE! I USED THE A.T.A.C. HOLO-PROJECTOR THEY ASSIGNED YOU.
IT'S ONLY GOOD FOR A FEW MOMENTS, BUT IT WAS ENOUGH TO DISTRACT THE SUSPECT.

HOW MANY SECRET AGENTS WERE ASSIGNED TO THIS CASE?!
GOOD QUESTION.

I'M TOO YOUNG TO BE AN AGENT.
BUT I AM IN THE TRAINING PROGRAM!
ID CODE
PASSWORD
TRAINEE

AS THE COMPETITION CONTINUES INSIDE THE STADIUM, THE AUTHORITIES HAVE COME TO TAKE THE CRIMINAL AWAY...

WHY DIDN'T ANYONE TELL US ALL THE DETAILS OF THIS CASE BEFORE HAND, DAD?

THANKS FOR TRUSTING ME WITH SUCH AN AWESOME ASSIGNMENT, MR. H.
CALL ME WHENEVER YOU NEED ME!
SMEK!
ER... OF COURSE, LINDSAY. AND GOOD JOB!
DON'T BE STRANGERS, GUYS!
WHEREVER YOU HEAR THE ROAR OF THE CROWD, YOU CAN BE SURE I'LL BE NEARBY!
NOW LET'S SEE ABOUT GETTING THE TWO OF YOU INTO YOUR REGULAR CLOTHES.
ACTUALLY, I THINK THIS NEW LOOK IS WORKING FOR ME...!

EPILOGUE: "HERE'S TO USING YOUR HEAD..."

WHAT THE HECK?
THAT WASN'T THERE WHEN I WENT TO SLEEP.
KEWL.
I WONDER HOW IT GOT HERE?
IT'S AN EXTRA ONE OF MINE.
I THOUGHT YOU COULD USE ONE.
I KNOW THAT VOICE...

WHAT'S UP, FRANK? COULDN'T RESIST THE CHANCE TO STOP BY AND MAKE FUN OF ME?
NOT AT ALL, BRIAN.
I JUST HATE THE THOUGHT OF SOMETHING HAPPENING TO YOU.

I'D HAVE TO FIND A WHOLE OTHER BONE-HEADED JOCK TO MAKE MY LIFE MISERABLE.
GOOD NIGHT, CONRAD.

HARDY, WAIT.
THE LIGHT KIND OF BOTHERS MY EYES STILL. AND... AND I NEED TO STUDY FOR MY EXAM ON MONDAY...

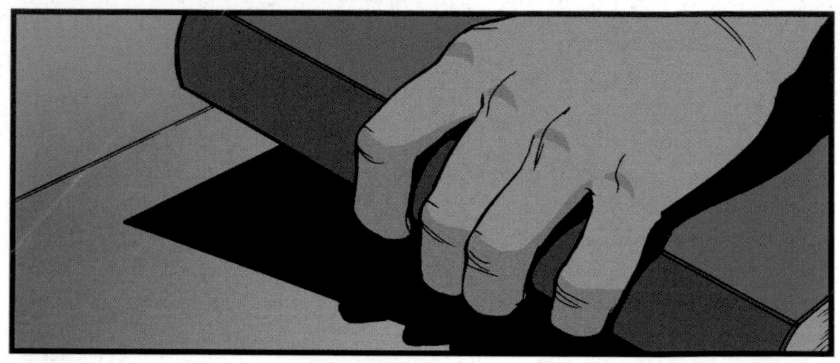

THE ELEMENTAL TABLE, RIGHT?
YES.
OKAY. WHAT'S THE SIGN FOR TERBIUM?

OH, MAN. YOU COULDN'T START OFF WITH AN EASY ONE?
LIKE ADAMANTIUM?
THAT'S NOT A REAL METAL...
HOSPITAL
THE END.

"HALEY DANELLE'S TOP EIGHT"
WOOHOO!
LOOK AT HIM GO!
DANCE, JOE! DANCE!
THANKS--I THINK I WILL!
CHAPTER ONE: "SATURDAY NIGHT DEAD!"

HE'S, LIKE, THE MOST AMAZING DANCER!
SERIOUS! THE DANCE MACHINE IS GOING TO GIVE UP BEFORE HE DOES!
MACHINE

FORGET EYE/HAND COORDINATION! CHECK OUT HIS LEG/FOOT COORDINATION!
I WISH I COULD DANCE LIKE THAT!
I CAN'T BELIEVE ALL THIS... AND HE ONLY PUT IN ONE DOLLAR!
HE MAKES IT ALL LOOK SO EASY!

"EASY"? HA!
THIS IS THE HARDEST, MOST DEMANDING DANCING I'VE EVER HAD TO DO!
I'M READY TO PASS OUT.
BUT I DON'T DARE!
BECAUSE IF I STOP DANCING, EVERYONE IN THIS ROOM...*DIES!*
AT THAT MOMENT, NOT AT ALL FAR AWAY...
CAN YOU HEAR ME, JOE?
YES, FRANK-- EVEN OVER THE SOUND OF THIS MUSIC.
HOLD ON A FEW MORE MOMENTS, AND I'LL USE THESE A.T.A.C.* TOOLS...
*A.T.A.C.: AMERICAN TEENS AGAINST CRIME.

... TO DISARM THIS BOMB ONCE AND FOR ALL.
BUT YOU CAN'T AFFORD TO MISS A SINGLE DANCE STEP --
-- BECAUSE IF YOUR FEET MISS A MOVE ON THE PLATFORM...?
THEN I EXPLODE ON THE CLUB SCENE, LITERALLY.
I HEAR YOU.
I WOULD HAVE PASSED OUT BY NOW!
UMM... HE'S BEEN DANCING FOR A WHILE.
I HEAR *THAT* TOO!

KLP!
PHEW!
UM... GOOD "PHEW"? OR BAD "PHEW"?
AN "I-DID-IT" PHEW.
THEN LET ME BE THE FIRST TO SAY...
TA DA!
CLAP CLAP CLAP
THANK YOU VERY MUCH! THANK YOU!
YOU RULE!

--TRAPPED?!

I THOUGHT THERE WAS AN ALLEY BACK HERE, BUT IT'S JUST A COURTYARD!

DON'T WORRY, MR. TALBOT. WE'RE WILLING TO HELP YOU OUT OF HERE.
AND INTO A JAIL CELL WHERE YOU BELONG.
YOU D-DON'T UNDERSTAND. I ONLY DID IT FOR THE INSURANCE.
I D-DIDN'T WANT TO HURT ANY OF THOSE K-KIDS.
WITH ALL DUE RESPECT, SIR, SAVE IT FOR THE AUTHORITIES.
I'M PUTTING IN A CALL TO OUR A.T.A.C. BACK-UP RIGHT NOW.

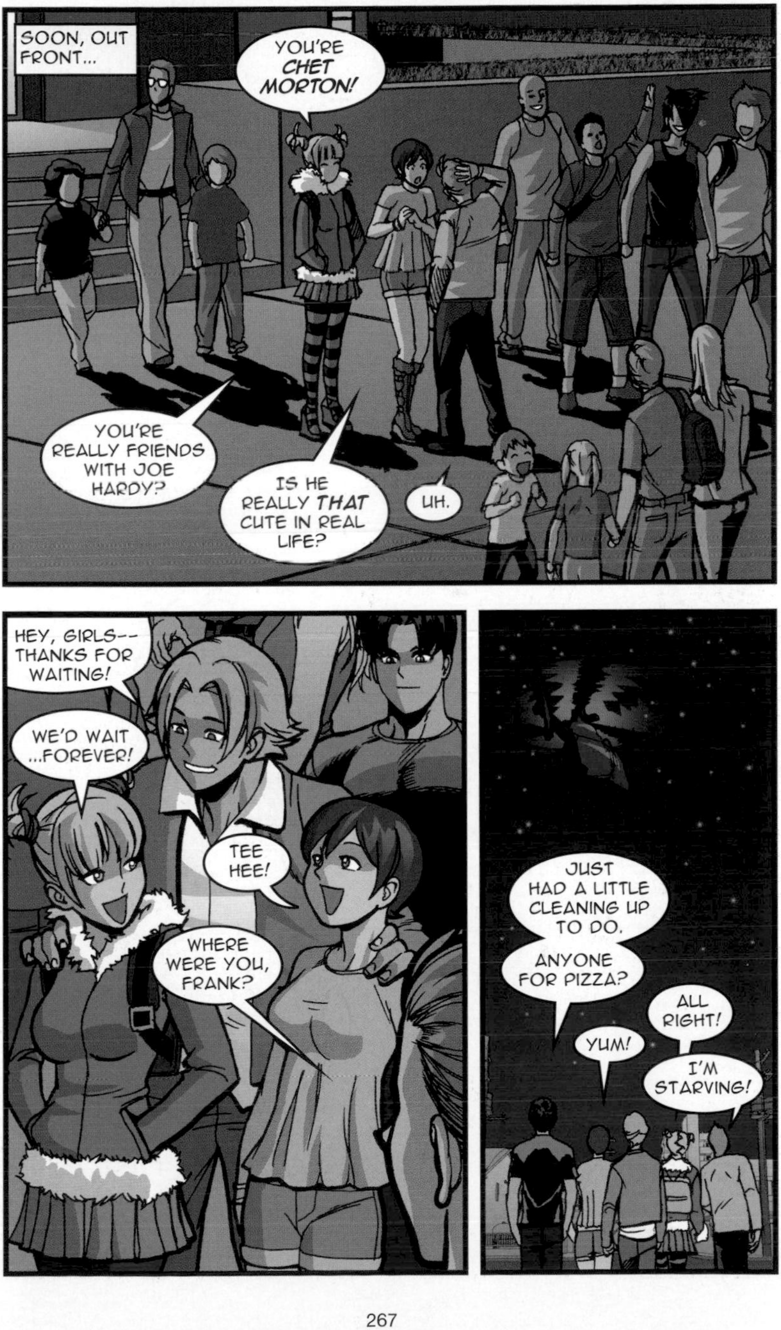

SOON, OUT FRONT...

YOU'RE *CHET MORTON!*

YOU'RE REALLY FRIENDS WITH JOE HARDY?

IS HE REALLY *THAT* CUTE IN REAL LIFE?

UH.

CHAPTER TWO: "DON'T CLICK ON ME!"

SURE, THEY LIVE A LIFE OF ACTION AND ADVENTURE...

...BUT AT THE END OF THE DAY, JOE AND FRANK HARDY ARE STILL JUST TWO REGULAR GUYS.

WHICH MEANS THEY ARE MEMBERS OF THE WORLD'S MOST POPULAR WEBSITE.

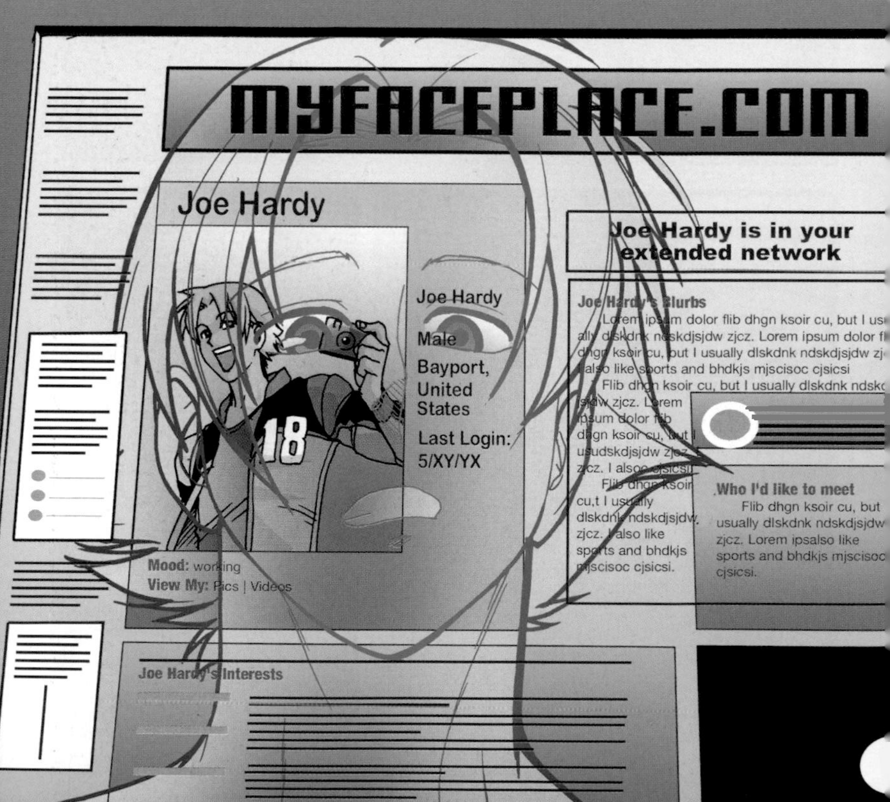

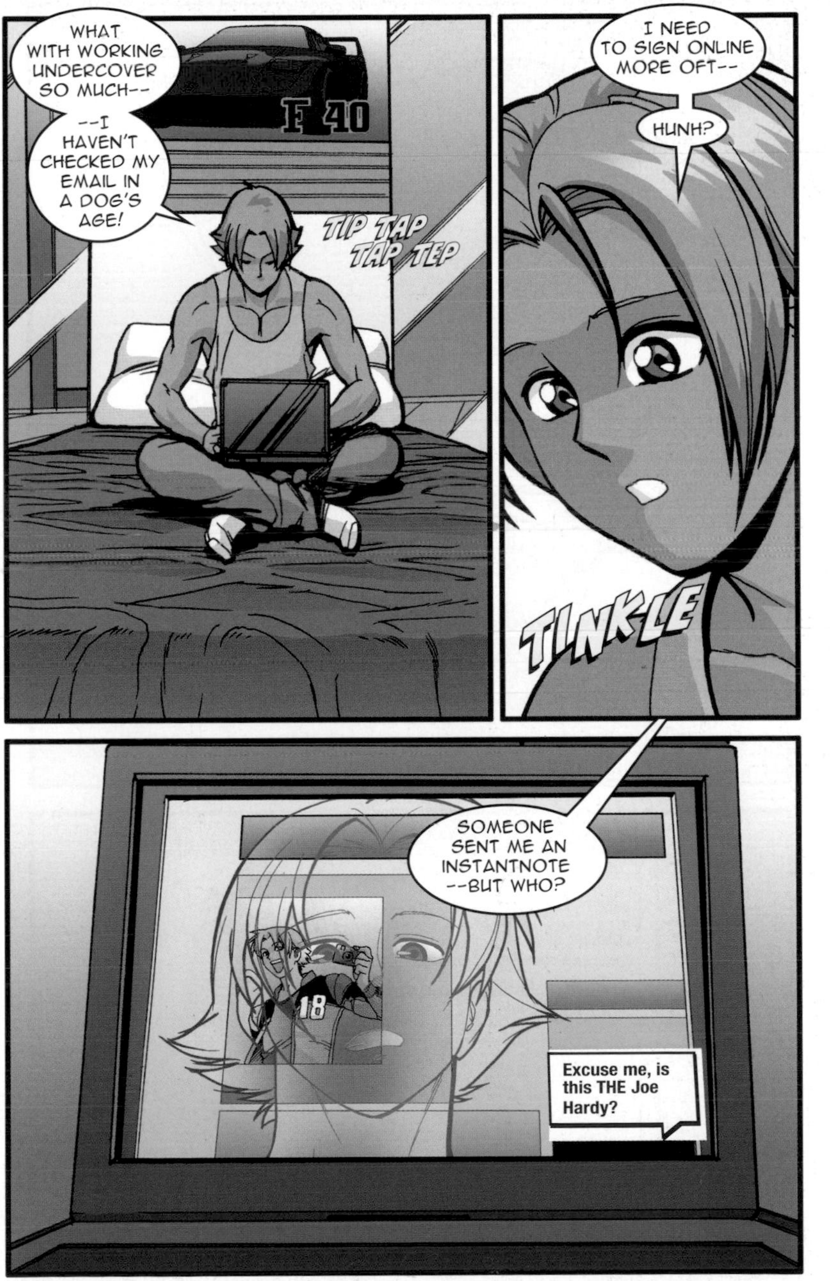

WHAT WITH WORKING UNDERCOVER SO MUCH--
--I HAVEN'T CHECKED MY EMAIL IN A DOG'S AGE!
TIP TAP TAP TEP
I NEED TO SIGN ONLINE MORE OFT--
HUNH?
TINKLE

NONE OTHER.

AND WHO IS THIS, MAY I ASK?

TIP TAP TAP

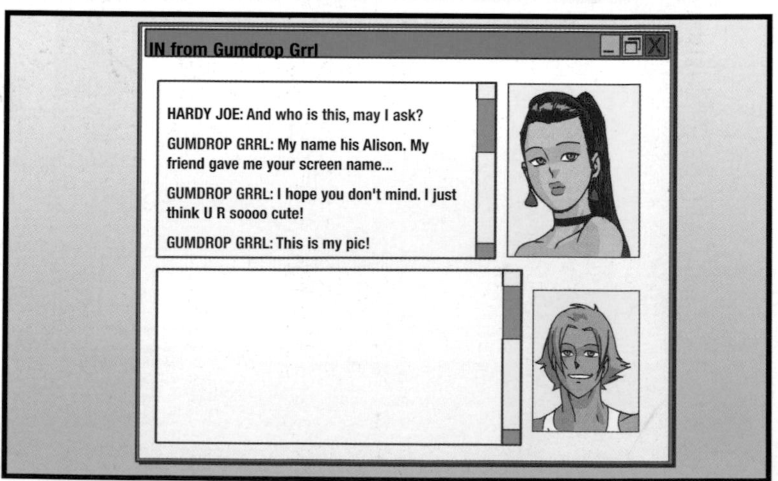

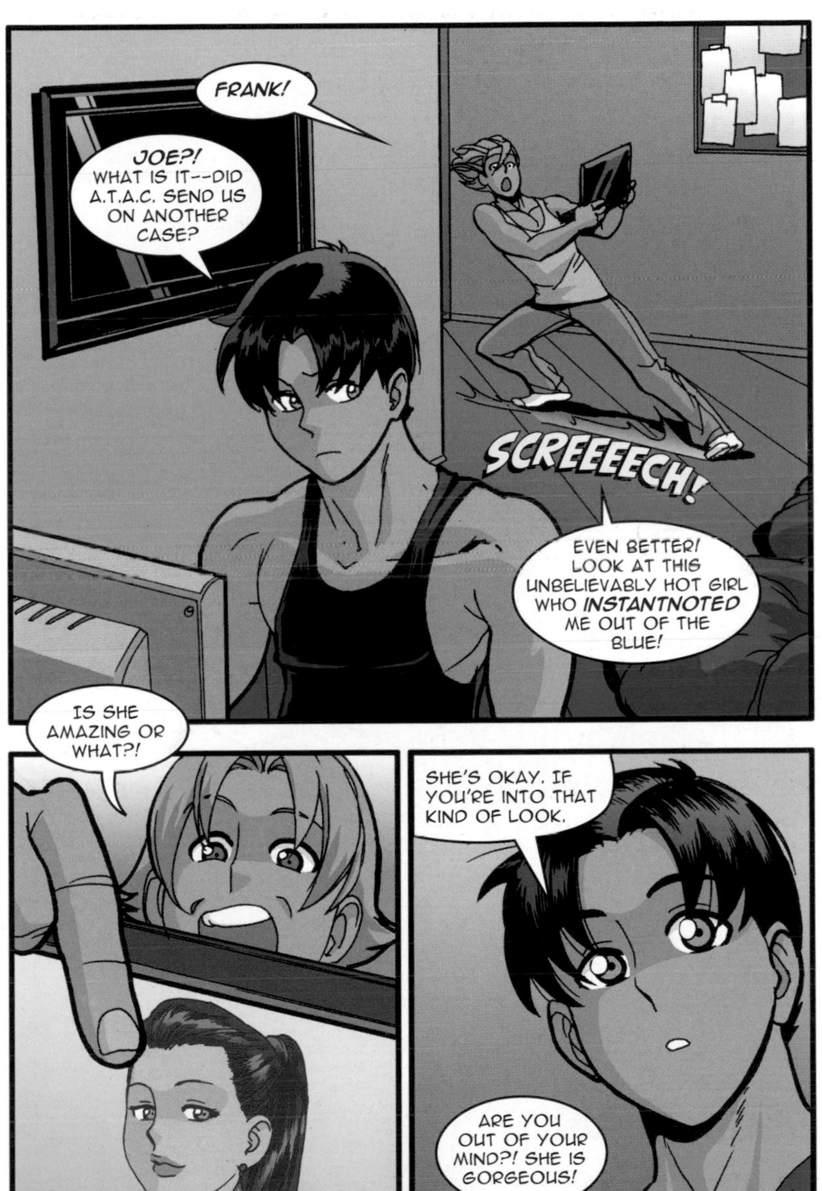
FRANK!
JOE?! WHAT IS IT--DID A.T.A.C. SEND US ON ANOTHER CASE?
SCREEEECH!
EVEN BETTER! LOOK AT THIS UNBELIEVABLY HOT GIRL WHO INSTANTNOTED ME OUT OF THE BLUE!
IS SHE AMAZING OR WHAT?!
SHE'S OKAY. IF YOU'RE INTO THAT KIND OF LOOK.
ARE YOU OUT OF YOUR MIND?! SHE IS GORGEOUS!

I'M GOING TO ASK HER OUT ON--HEY!
WHY IS SHE ON YOUR SCREEN TOO?!
WOW. YOU'RE RIGHT.
I DIDN'T EVEN NOTICE.
OH, REAL FUNNY! WHERE DID YOU GET THAT PIC?

HA HA! I JUST DOWN-LOADED IT OFF A WEBSITE.

"NONE OTHER!" YOU ARE SO SLICK--IT'S HYSTERI-CAL!

I KNEW IT WAS TOO GOOD TO BE REAL.
"I JUST THINK U R SOOOO CUTE!"

CHAPTER THREE: "DRIVE-IN ME CRAZY!"

LATER THAT NIGHT...

...AT THE BAYPORT DRIVE-IN...

IT SEEMS LIKE THE WHOLE TOWN HAS SHOWN UP FOR THE FRIDAY NIGHT MOVIE!

THIS IS FUN, FRANK--LIKE WE'RE WATCHING THE WORLD'S LARGEST FLAT-SCREEN TV!

NO! THAT IS NOT FAIR! I'M TOO WEAK FROM HUNGER TO GET MORE.

TOO WEAK... MUST EAT.

MUST... POP... CORN.

OKAY, OKAY-- I'LL GO!

AND I'LL PICK YOU UP YOUR OSCAR WHILE I'M OUT THERE.

THANK YOU, THANK YOU...

...AND THANK YOU TO THE MEMBERS OF THE ACADEMY. HEH.

SORRY. BROTHER OR NOT, THAT LINE IS MUCH TOO LONG.
I'LL GO REFILL THE POPCORN IN A LITTLE --
YEAH, YEAH--HA HA.
I GET IT.

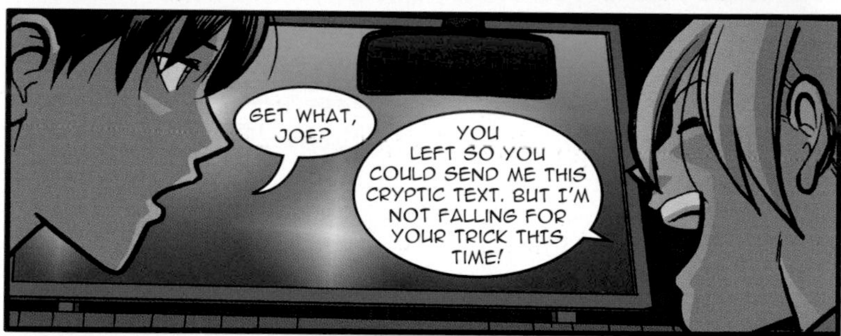
GET WHAT, JOE?
YOU LEFT SO YOU COULD SEND ME THIS CRYPTIC TEXT. BUT I'M NOT FALLING FOR YOUR TRICK THIS TIME!

JOE.
I DIDN'T SEND THAT.
YOU MEAN...?
SOMEONE IS REALLY IN TROUBLE?

A FEW MOMENTS LATER....

THIS NEXT TEXT TOLD US TO COME TO THE PLAYGROUND NEAR THE DRIVE-IN...

BUT NOBODY IS HERE. EVERYONE IS WATCHING THE MOVIE.

IT STOPPED.
BUT IT HAS TO BE OUR MYSTERY TEXTER --IT HAS TO BE.
I AGREE. IN CASE IT'S A TRAP WE HAVE TO BE READY FOR ANYTHING.
ANYTHING BUT THE MOST WELL APPORTIONED TREEHOUSE IN THE HISTORY OF TREE-HOUSES?! 
I COULD MOVE IN HERE TOMORROW AND DIE A HAPPY KID-- LOOK AT THOSE GAME SYSTEMS! THEY'RE STATE OF THE ART!

YOU'RE HERE! YOU'RE HERE!
?!
I KNEW IT! I KNEW IF I SENT YOU THAT TEXT THAT YOU'D COME HELP ME!
OMG! I KNEW YOU'D BE ABLE TO SAVE US!
"US"?
ME AND MY FRIENDS!

UM... DO I KNOW YOU?
OH, SORRY. MY NAME IS HALEY DANELLE. AND I KNOW THIS IS PROBABLY AGAINST EVERY RULE IN THE BOOK--
--BUT I CONTACTED YOU BECAUSE... WELL...
... BECAUSE I KNOW YOU TWO ARE SPECIAL AGENTS FOR A.T.A.C. AND I COULDN'T THINK OF ANYONE ELSE TO CALL!
?!?

DON'T WORRY, REALLY! I PROMISE I WON'T TELL ANYONE!
WE BELIEVE YOU, HALEY... I--
YOU MIGHT, BUT I--
...WE JUST WANT TO KNOW HOW YOU FOUND OUT ABOUT THE AMERICAN TEENS AGAINST CRIME?

WELL, COMPUTERS ARE SORT OF MY HOBBY. MOSTLY I TRAIN WITH MY HORSE ZOEY.
AS YOU KNOW, A.T.A.C. RECRUITS TEENS WITH CER-TAIN SPECIALTIES FOR CERTAIN CASES.

"LAST YEAR I WAS ASKED TO HELP BREAK UP A TEEN HORSE RUSTLING RING.
"WHEN MY FRIENDS AND I GOT IN THIS PREDICAMENT, I HACKED INTO A.T.A.C.'S FILES AND LEARNED ABOUT YOU TWO!

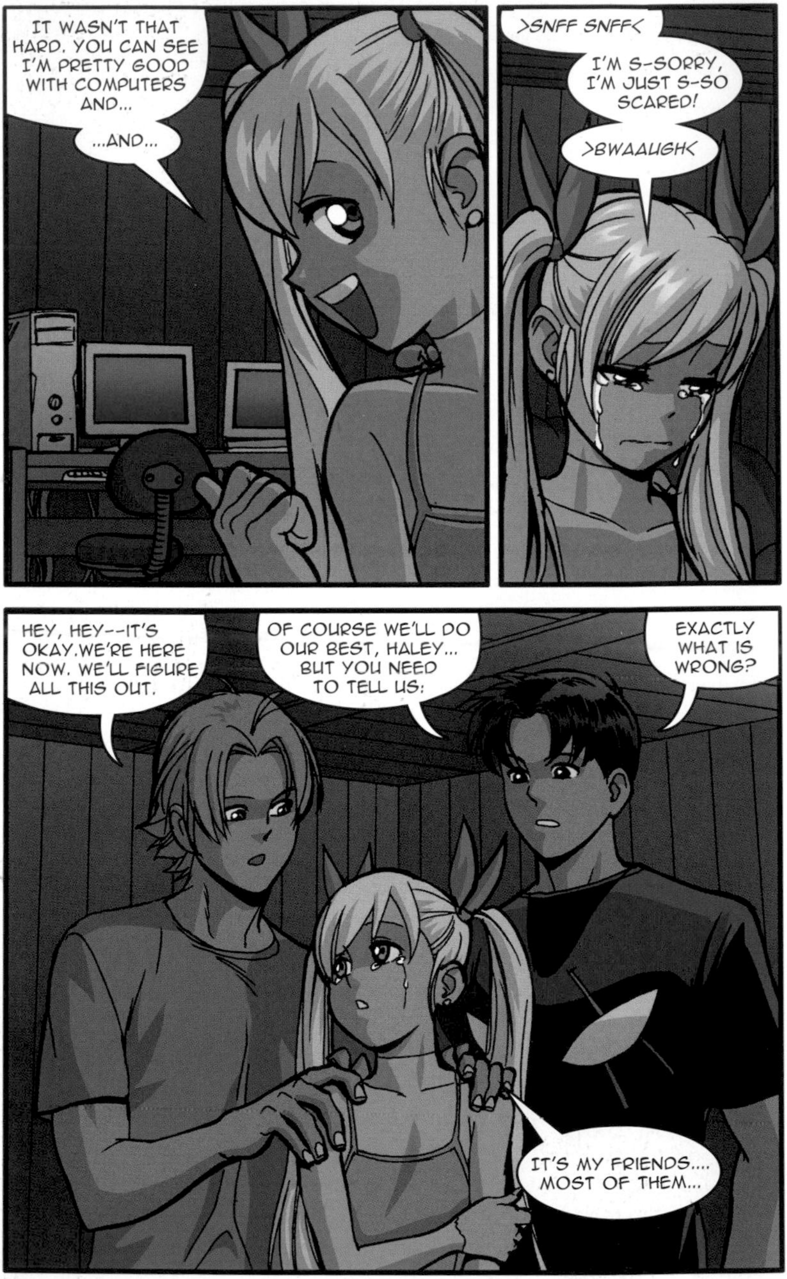

HEY, HEY--IT'S OKAY.WE'RE HERE NOW. WE'LL FIGURE ALL THIS OUT.

OF COURSE WE'LL DO OUR BEST, HALEY... BUT YOU NEED TO TELL US:

EXACTLY WHAT IS WRONG?

IT'S MY FRIENDS.... MOST OF THEM...

CHAPTER FOUR: "FRIENDS OF DOOM!"

MYFACEPLACE.COM

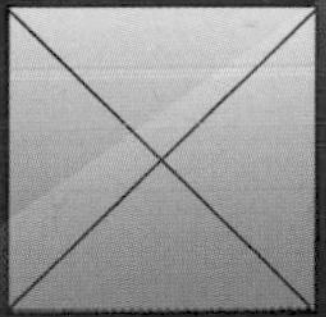

HALEY DANELLE, START FROM THE BEGINNING. WHY DO YOU THINK SOMEONE IS TAKING ALL YOUR FRIENDS?

"BECAUSE THEY ARE! ME, KAITLYN, RACHEL, OLIVA ...AT SCHOOL WE'RE INSEPARABLE!

"THAT MEANS WE HANG OUT TOGETHER ALL THE TIME.

"WE'RE NOT A CLIQUE. WE'RE NOT MEAN GIRLS. WE'RE JUST BEST FRIENDS!

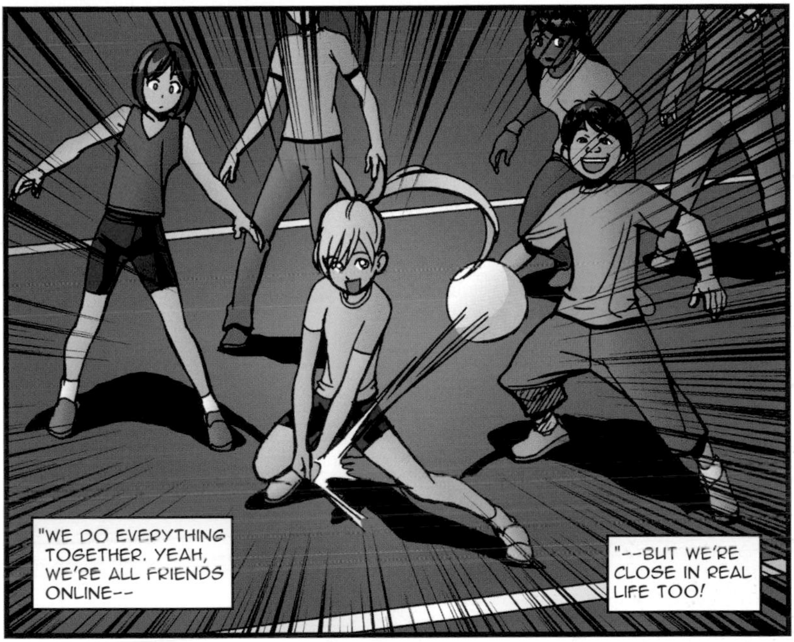

"WE DO EVERYTHING TOGETHER. YEAH, WE'RE ALL FRIENDS ONLINE--

"--BUT WE'RE CLOSE IN REAL LIFE TOO!

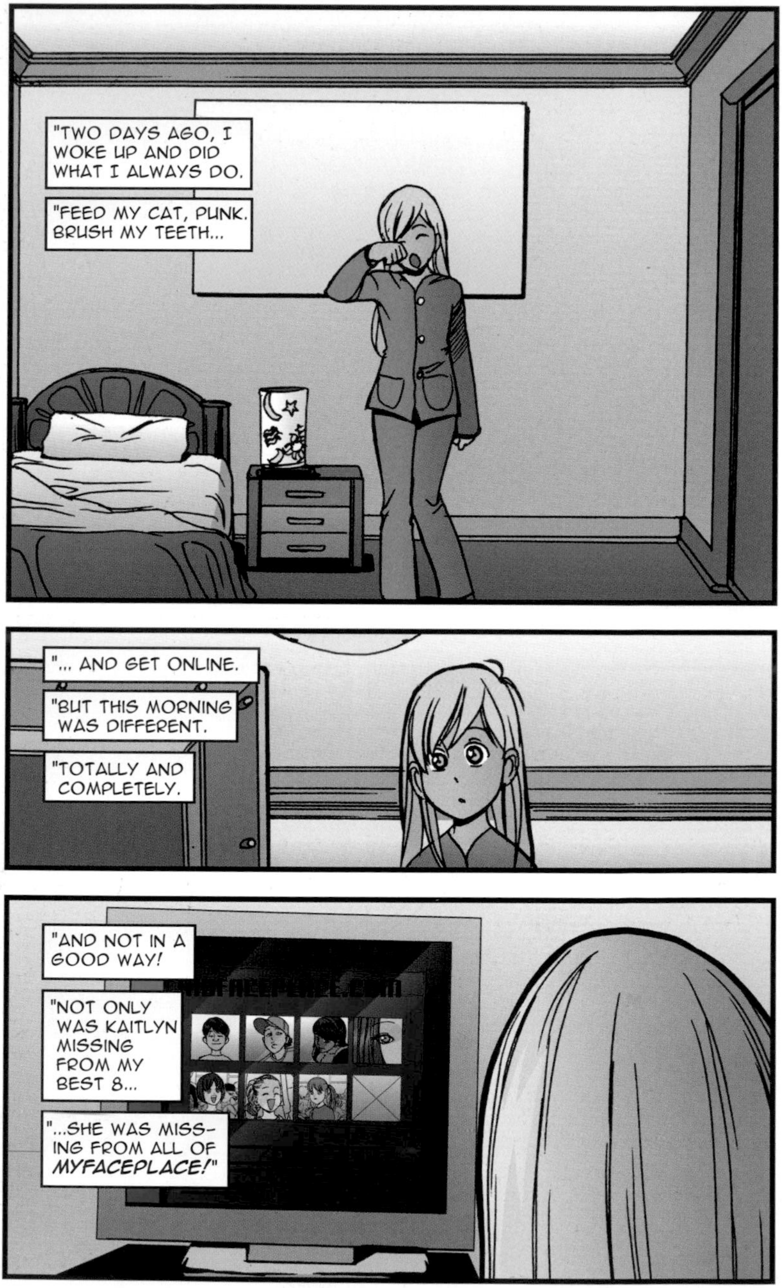

"TWO DAYS AGO, I WOKE UP AND DID WHAT I ALWAYS DO.

"FEED MY CAT, PUNK. BRUSH MY TEETH...

IS IT POSSIBLE YOU TWO GOT INTO A FIGHT AND YOU DON'T--
NO! SHE'S MISSING! SOMETHING HAPPENED TO HER!
NOBODY HAS SEEN HER SINCE BAND REHEARSAL!
OKAY. YOU'VE CONVINCED US.
LET ME JUST POKE AROUND A LITTLE IN CYBERSPACE AND SEE IF WE CAN'T PICK UP SOME CLUES.
TAKKATIKKA TAP TIKKA
OKAY, BUT YOU HAVE TO HURRY! I'M REALLY--
--WORRIED, AND THAT'S COMPLETELY UNDERSTANDABLE. BUT YOU CONTACTED US TO HELP YOU, SO YOU HAVE TO TRUST US TO FIND YOUR FRIENDS.

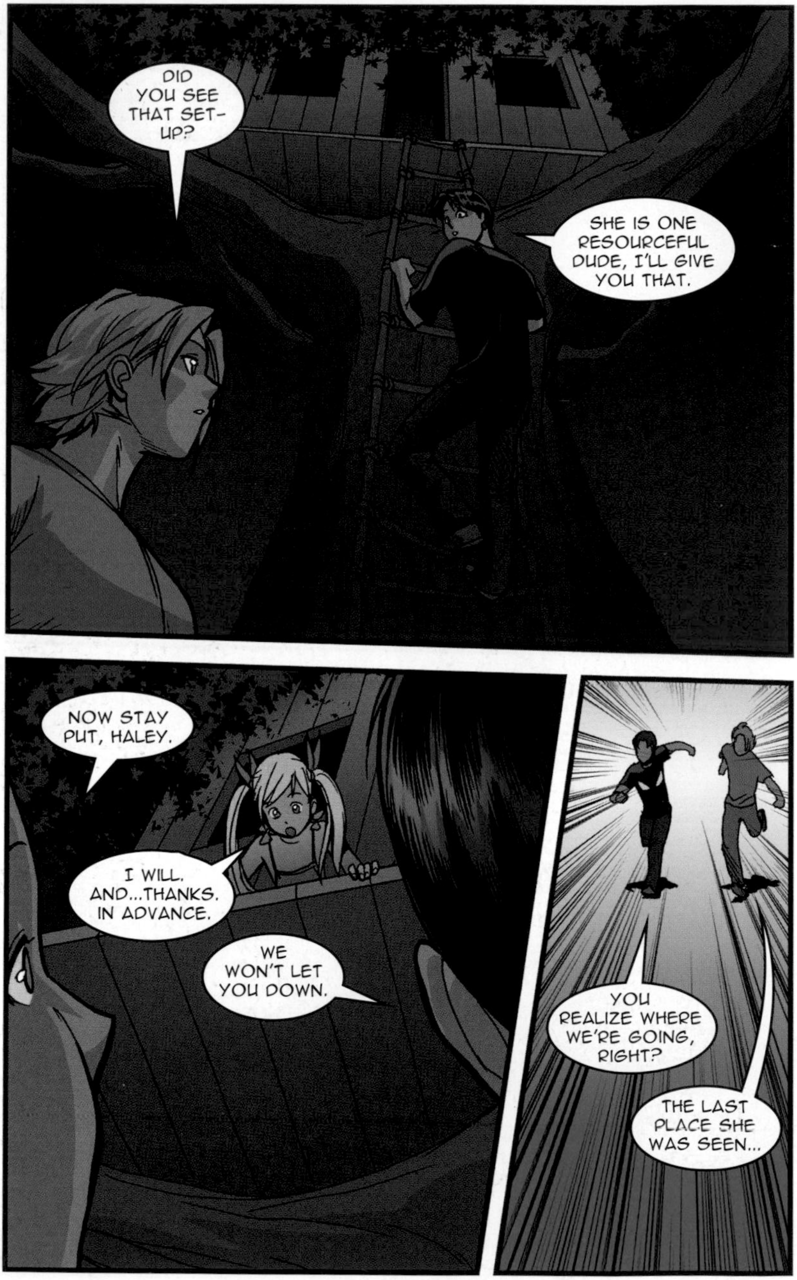

DID YOU SEE THAT SET-UP?
SHE IS ONE RESOURCEFUL DUDE, I'LL GIVE YOU THAT.
NOW STAY PUT, HALEY.
I WILL. AND...THANKS. IN ADVANCE.
WE WON'T LET YOU DOWN.
YOU REALIZE WHERE WE'RE GOING, RIGHT?
THE LAST PLACE SHE WAS SEEN...

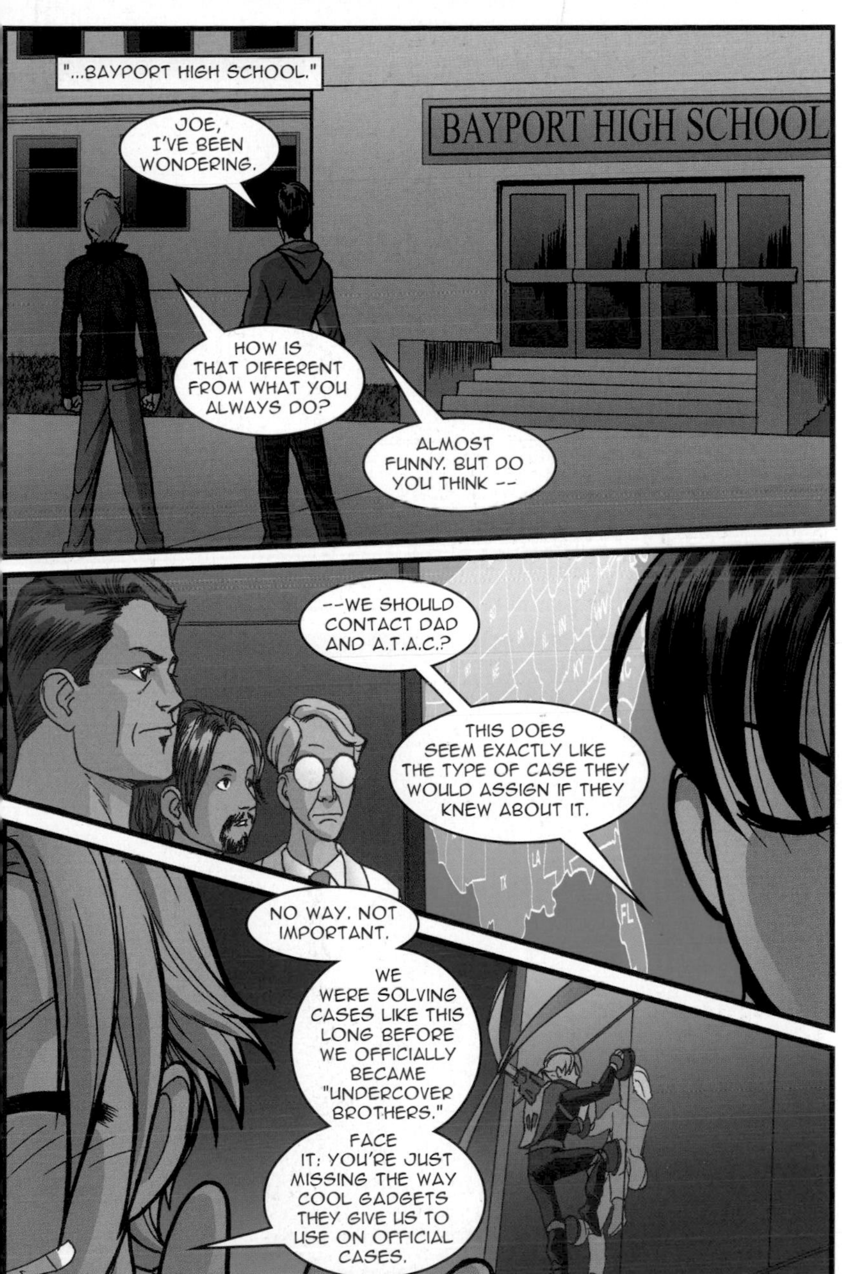
"...BAYPORT HIGH SCHOOL."
BAYPORT HIGH SCHOOL
JOE, I'VE BEEN WONDERING.
HOW IS THAT DIFFERENT FROM WHAT YOU ALWAYS DO?
ALMOST FUNNY. BUT DO YOU THINK --
--WE SHOULD CONTACT DAD AND A.T.A.C.?
THIS DOES SEEM EXACTLY LIKE THE TYPE OF CASE THEY WOULD ASSIGN IF THEY KNEW ABOUT IT.
NO WAY. NOT IMPORTANT.
WE WERE SOLVING CASES LIKE THIS LONG BEFORE WE OFFICIALLY BECAME "UNDERCOVER BROTHERS."
FACE IT: YOU'RE JUST MISSING THE WAY COOL GADGETS THEY GIVE US TO USE ON OFFICIAL CASES.

A LASER-POWERED LOCK PICK WOULD CERTAINLY COME IN HANDY THIS MOMENT.
ADMIT IT.
PFFFT. YOU'RE GETTING LAZY, OLDER BROTHER.
"LAZY?!"
PLEASE.
TRY TO KEEP UP!
FWOSH!
FINE. SO WHAT ARE WE DOING HERE IN THESE BUSHES?
REMEMBER HOW YOU COMPLAINED LAST SEMESTER ABOUT YOUR SOCIAL STUDIES TEACHER?
"COMPLAINED"? I COMMENTED ON HIM, I DIDN'T COMPLAIN.

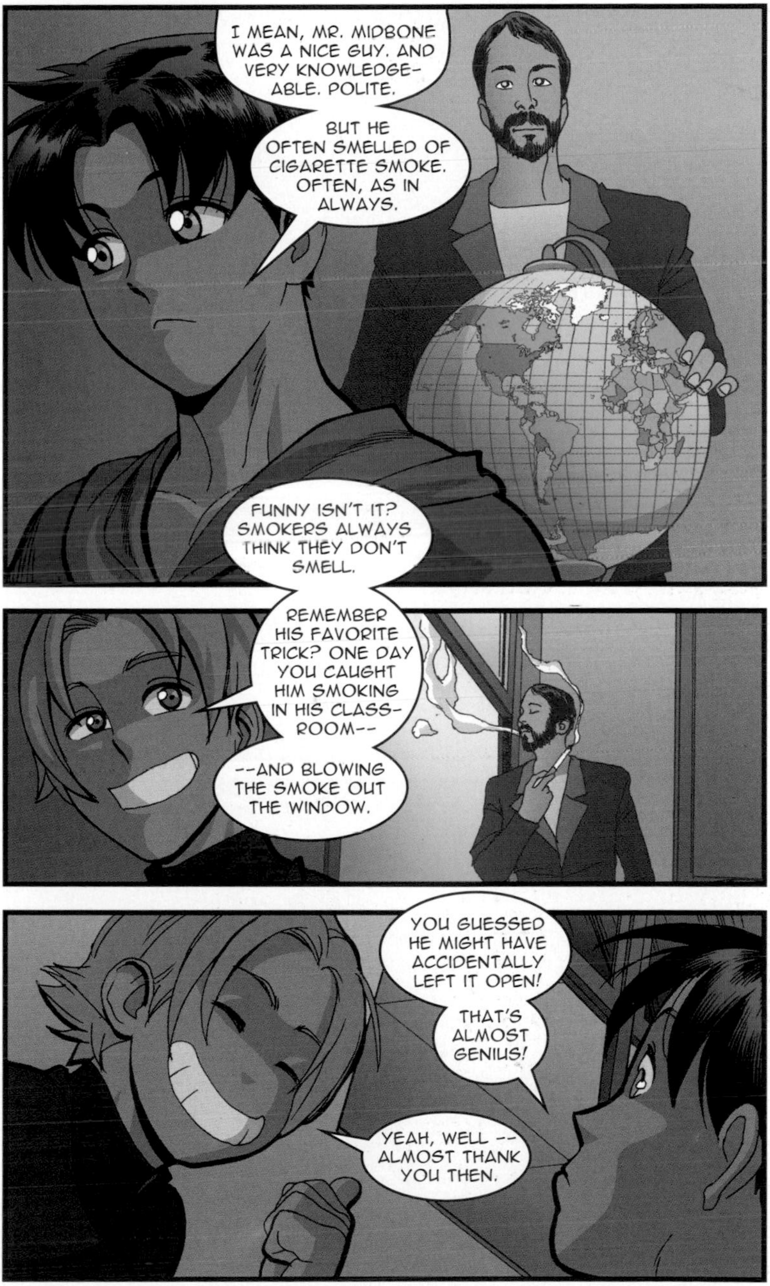

I MEAN, MR. MIDBONE WAS A NICE GUY. AND VERY KNOWLEDGE-ABLE. POLITE.
BUT HE OFTEN SMELLED OF CIGARETTE SMOKE. OFTEN, AS IN ALWAYS.
FUNNY ISN'T IT? SMOKERS ALWAYS THINK THEY DON'T SMELL.

THIS MUST BE THE PLACE.

UH, JOE. YOU KNOW WHERE THE BAND ROOM IS. YOU'VE BEEN TAKING DRUM LESSONS FOR TWO YEARS.
I KNOW. I WAS BEING DRAMATIC.

BUT SINCE THERE'S NO ONE HERE BUT THE INSTRUMENTS --
YOU WEREN'T PAYING ATTENTION WHEN WE LOOKED AT HER PROFILE.
--I'M NOT SURE WHAT CLUES YOU THINK WE'RE GOING TO FIND ABOUT KAITLYN.
SHE'S A BASSOON PLAYER. AND AN ACCOMPLISHED ONE AT THAT.

THAT ONE IS HERS.
NOW YOU'RE JUST SHOWING OFF.
THEY ALL LOOK EXACTLY THE SAME. HOW CAN YOU KNOW WHICH ONE IS HERS?

WOW!

CALM DOWN. IT'S NOT THAT IMPRESSIVE I KNEW THAT.

NO, "WOW" AS IN --

CHAPTER FIVE:
"AND THE BAND SLAYED ON!"
--GET OUT OF THE WAY--WE'RE ABOUT TO BE CRUSHED BY A RUNAWAY PIANO!
OH. NOW I SEE THE SUBTLE DIFFERENCE.

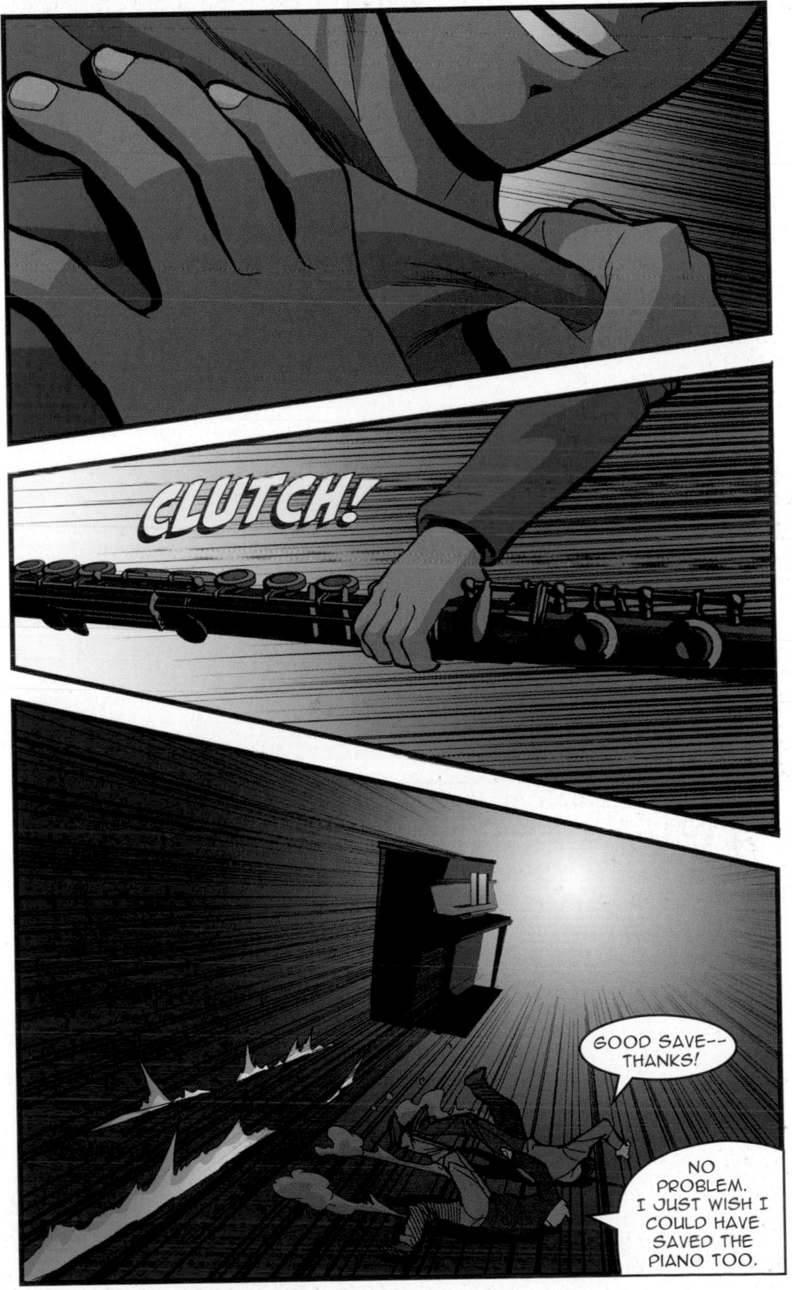
CLUTCH!
GOOD SAVE--
THANKS!
NO PROBLEM. I JUST WISH I COULD HAVE SAVED THE PIANO TOO.

-- KA Bong --
YOU THINK HE HEARD THAT?
AUNT TRUDY HEARD THAT AND SHE'S AT HOME IN BED!

SOON...
I KNOW WE'RE TRYING TO FIND THOSE MISSING KIDS --

--BUT I FEEL A LITTLE BAD FOR THAT JANITOR.
HE'S GOING TO HAVE A LOT OF EXPLAINING TO DO IN THE MORNING
?!
WE'LL GET DAD TO EXPLAIN IT TOSHERIFF COLLIG AND HE'LL EXPLAIN IT TO THE PRINCIPAL AND EVERYTHING WILL BE FINE.

I ONLY WISH WE SAW THE PERSON WHO TRIED TO CRUSH US WITH THAT PIANO.
YEAH, IT DIDN'T FEEL LIKE A COINCIDENCE, HUH?

CAN WE GO NOW?
JUST...A...
...MINUTE.

THAT'S IT! I KNOW EXACTLY WHERE SHE WAS SUPPOSED TO MEET THIS MYSTERY PERSON.

THEN LETS GO-- YOU CAN GLOAT ON THE WAY!

I CAN'T SEE YOU TWO, BUT I KNOW YOU'RE UP THERE!
COME DOWN HERE AND FACE UP TO YOUR RESPONSIBILITY FOR--

--FOR... DISAPPEARING?!
B-BUT... BUT I HEARD SOMEBODY!

DIDN'T I?
MAN, I SO HAVE TO APPLY FOR A JOB ON THE DAY SHIFT!

LATER, ON THE OTHER SIDE OF TOWN...?

JAVA

A COFFEE SHOP?

I DON'T GET IT.

BECAUSE YOU AREN'T AS HIP AS I AM.

NOW I GET IT.
"REGULAR" AS IN COFFEE...
...AS IN THE JAVA CAFE...
...AS IN THE HOTTEST CYBER CAFE IN THE CITY!
AND SINCE THIS CASE STARTED ON THE INTERNET--
--AND IT'S FILLED TO THE BRIM WITH TEENAGERS?
IT'S THE PERFECT PLACE TO LOOK FOR THE PERSON WHO SLIPPED KAITLYN THAT NOTE.

WHILE I'M ON A ROLL...
...I'M GOING TO GUESS THAT'S TTM...
"THOMAS THE MODERATOR"-- FROM MYFACEPLACE! PERFECT.
HI, THOMAS. I'M JOE HARDY--THIS IS MY BROTHER, FRANK.
HELLO, GUYS! WELCOME TO JAVA!

I CAN EXPLAIN EVERYTHING...!
WHY YOU SLIPPED KAITLYN A NOTE IN BAND CLASS?
WHERE SHE AND THE OTHER GIRLS ARE?
NO AND NO. BUT I CAN TELL YOU THE ONE THING I DO KNOW--
--THAT'S NOT MY SIGNATURE!
IT'S MORE LIKE INITIALS.

JOE, DO WE BELIEVE HIM?
IF NOT, IT WAS THE MOST ORIGINAL LIE I'VE EVER HEARD.
I'M TELLING YOU THE TRUTH! LOOK AROUND!
I'M TRYING TO EXPAND THE JAVA CAFE--BY ADDING ON WITH CONSTRUCTION AND REDOING THE BASE-MENT.
"THE CHAT ROOM" IS GOING TO BE EVEN COOLER! I'M GOING TO RENT IT OUT FOR PRIVATE PARTIES.
DON'T YOU SEE--?
CHAT ROOM

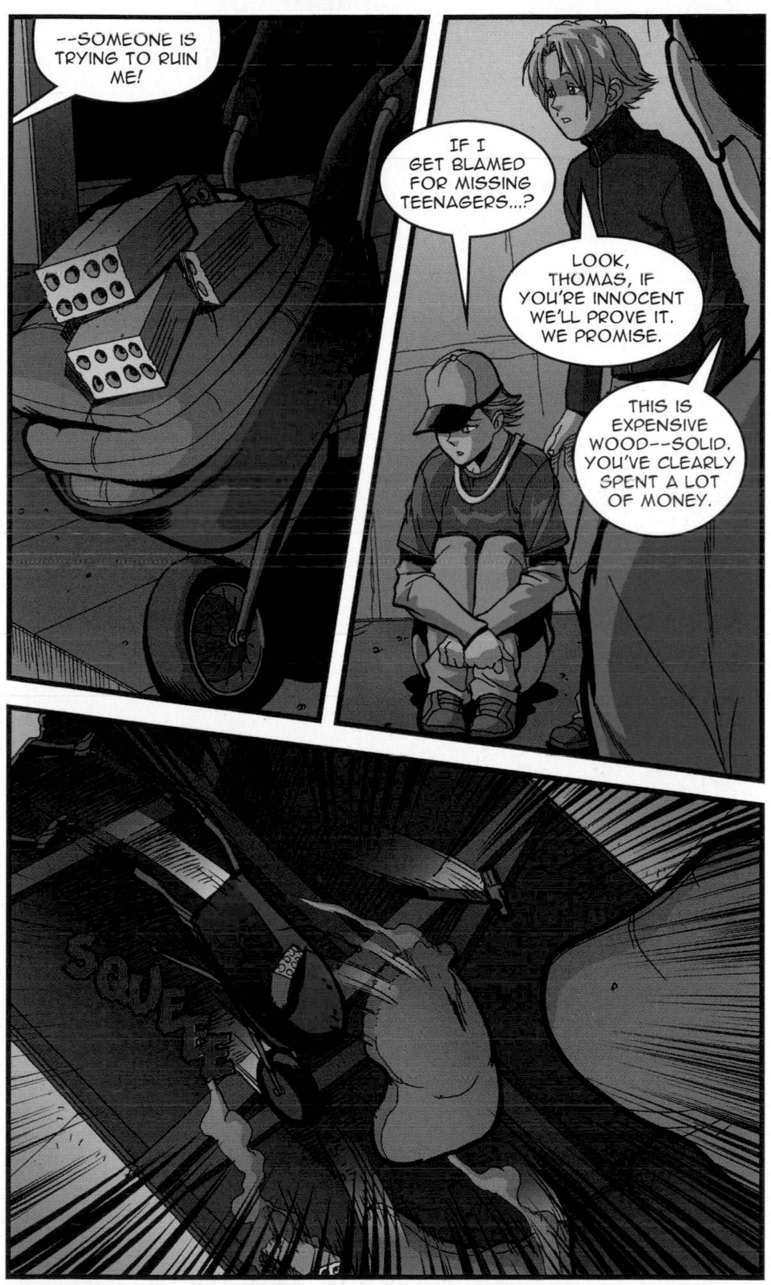
--SOMEONE IS TRYING TO RUIN ME!
IF I GET BLAMED FOR MISSING TEENAGERS...?
LOOK, THOMAS, IF YOU'RE INNOCENT WE'LL PROVE IT. WE PROMISE.
THIS IS EXPENSIVE WOOD--SOLID. YOU'VE CLEARLY SPENT A LOT OF MONEY.

UM...!
WE SEE IT!
CHAPTER SIX:
"I CEMENT TO KILL YOU ALL!"

JOE--HERE! *NOW!*
WILL THIS PLANK HOLD?!
IF THE BAGS HIT AT THE PROPER ANGLE OF THE WOOD--
PUFT!
PUFT!
POOFT!
--THEN I DON'T SEE WHY NOT?

-COUGH!-
-GAK!-
WHERE'RE YOU... GOING?
THIS IS THE SECOND TIME TONIGHT SOMEONE HAS TRIED TO HURT US...!
...IT'S TIME TO RETURN THE FAVOR!
DEEP BREATHS, JOE. IT'S NOT OUR PLACE TO HURT ANYONE WE DON'T HAVE TO!
THOUGH I GUESS THE POINT IS MOOT THIS VERY MINUTE.
WHOEVER ATTACKED US--AGAIN --IS GONE!

I GUESS THE ONLY THING WE KNOW MOSTLY FOR SURE IS...
...THOMAS DIDN'T HAVE ANYTHING TO DO WITH THOSE MISSING GIRLS.
DON'T LOOK SO DOWN, JOE --
--WE'VE STILL GOT CLUES O' PLENTY TO HELP US FIND THE OTHERS.
MY PERSONAL COMPUTER? YOU BROUGHT IT WITH YOU?
OF COURSE. ALWAYS COME PREPARED.
PREPARED WITH MY COMPUTER?
KAITLYN HAD A PIC OF HER PLAY-ING BASSOON.
THIS PIC OF RACHEL SHOWS HER SINGING IN A CONCERT IN THE PARK.
SO THEN --

"--IT'S OFF TO DIXON PARK WE GO."

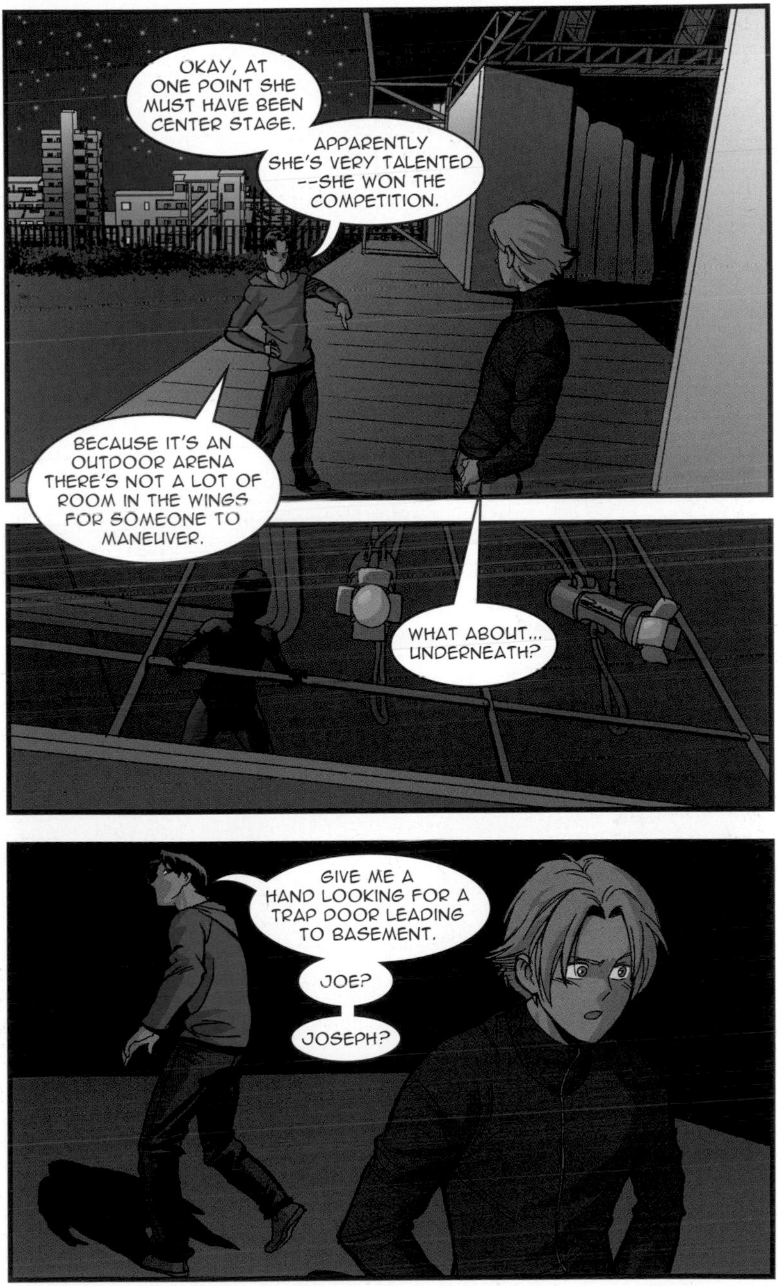

OKAY, AT ONE POINT SHE MUST HAVE BEEN CENTER STAGE.
APPARENTLY SHE'S VERY TALENTED --SHE WON THE COMPETITION.
BECAUSE IT'S AN OUTDOOR ARENA THERE'S NOT A LOT OF ROOM IN THE WINGS FOR SOMEONE TO MANEUVER.
WHAT ABOUT... UNDERNEATH?

LOOK, I WANT TO HELP BUT I REALLY REALLY REALLY HAVE TO GO TO THE BATHROOM!
DID I SAY "REALLY"?!
SO THEN GO!
NO HARM, NO FOUL.
I THINK I SAW ONE NEAR THE FOOD STANDS.
THANKS! I'LL BE BACK IN FIVE!
OKAY, STAGE.
GIVE UP YOUR SECRETS.

POINTS FOR CRAFTSMAN-SHIP.
I BARELY NOTICED THIS HANDLE.
CRE--
--EEEK!
JOE?
BACK ALREADY?

CHAPTER SEVEN: "JUST A STAGE..."
NOPE.
NOT JOE.

SPURKRASHK!

I DIDN'T REALLY GO TO THE BATHROOM!
WE SET THAT UP BEFORE HAND, FIGURING YOU WERE PROBABLY WATCHING US.

TWICE NOW YOU TRIED TO CRUSH US GOOD.

I TOLD FRANK YOU'D TRY AGAIN --ONLY THIS TIME WE'D BE READY.
SO WE SPLIT UP, AND I SNUCK BACK!

NOW THIS IS WHERE WE STOP YOU AND FREE THE GIRLS YOU TOOK!

IF YOU DON'T COME OVER HERE NOW, I'M JUST GOING TO --

WHA--WHY IS THIS CATWALK SO... SHAKY?

GIGGE LIGGA

YOU--YOU LOOSENED THE BOLTS?

YOU MUST HAVE FIGURED...

...MY EXTRA WEIGHT WOULD BE TOO MUCH!
I GIVE YOU POINTS FOR THAT.
THAT WAS THINKING AHEAD.
WHO AM I KIDDING?! NO TIME TO GIVE KUDOS--
--BEFORE I LAND. AND HARD!

FRANK!
LET YOUR BODY GO LIMP, JOE.
I GOT YOU.
WHAMMO!
UHN!
MPH!
YOU OKAY?
GREAT, MOSTLY. I HAVE TO SAY--IT HURT A LOT LESS THAN I THOUGHT IT WOULD.
SPEAK FOR YOURSELF, LUG.

NO SURPRISE THAT OUR SUSPECT IS LONG GONE.
OR MAYBE NOT SO LONG...

...MAYBE WE CAN STILL FIND--
NO, DON'T. THERE MIGHT BE AN EASIER WAY.

THIS PERSON IS METHODICAL. EVERY DETAIL SEEMS PLANNED.
OKAY.
MAYBE WE CAN USE THAT TO OUR ADVANTAGE.

NOT MUCH LATER...

...BACK AT THE JAVA...

YOU CAN PUT THAT COMPUTER AWAY, JOE.

WE'RE GONNA HIT THIS OLD SCHOOL:

PEN AND PAPER.

FROM WHAT WE'VE SEEN, THE PERSON RESPONSIBLE IS SYSTEMATICALLY GOING THROUGH HALEY'S LIST.

WE HAVEN'T FOUND ANY BODIES, WHICH MAKES ME THINK IT'S NOT MURDER.

NONE OF THEM SEEM OVERLY RICH. SO IT'S PROBABLY NOT A RANSOM SITUATION.
AND THERE'S NO NOTE.

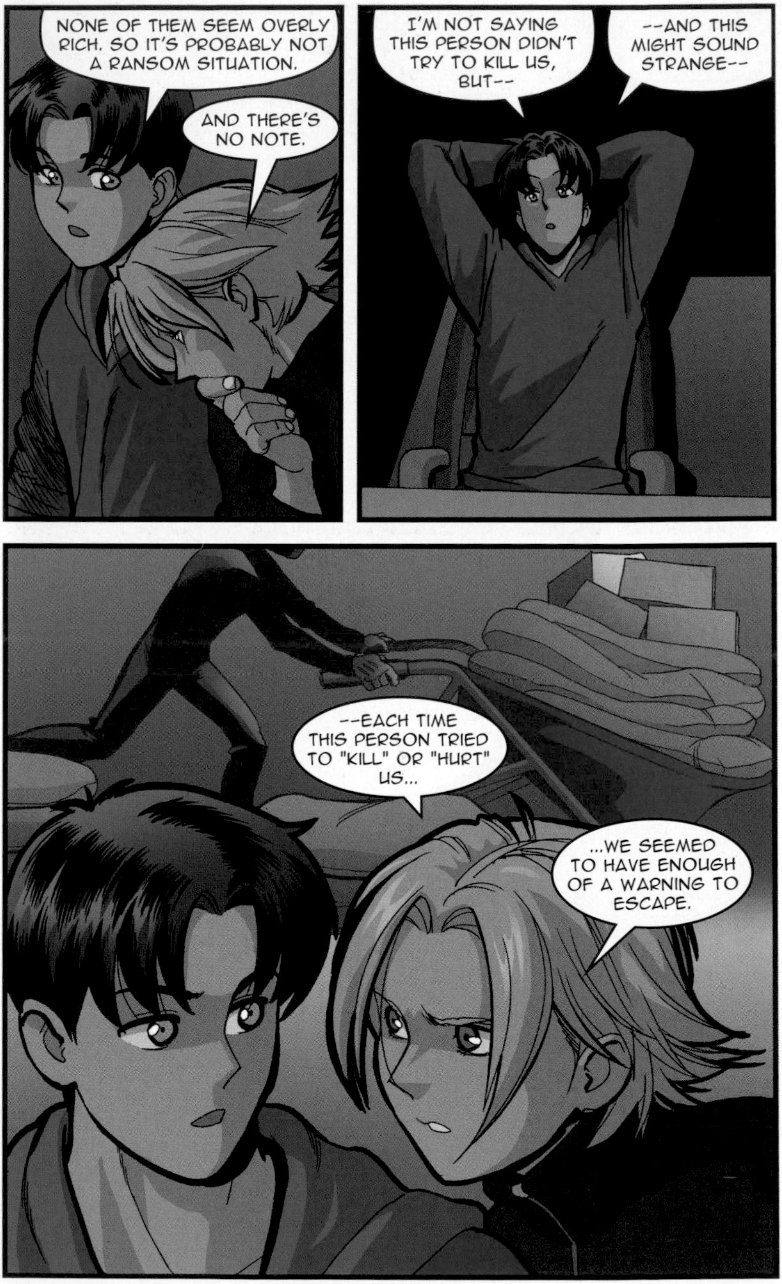

I'M NOT SAYING THIS PERSON DIDN'T TRY TO KILL US, BUT--
--AND THIS MIGHT SOUND STRANGE--

--EACH TIME THIS PERSON TRIED TO "KILL" OR "HURT" US...
...WE SEEMED TO HAVE ENOUGH OF A WARNING TO ESCAPE.

SOMEONE WHO DOESN'T WANT TO ACTUALLY HURT HALEY'S FRIENDS?
COULD THIS JUST BE A PRANK? LET'S LOOK AT HER FRIENDS AGAIN AND--

NO. THE ANSWER ISN'T ON THE INTERNET, JOE
IT'S NOT ONE OF HER FRIENDS...

?
I THINK IT'S SOMEONE WHO IS NOT HER FRIEND.
NOT AN ENEMY... JUST SOMEONE WHO HASN'T BEEN INVITED INTO HALEY'S CIRCLE OF FRIENDS.

"...WOULDN'T YOU START IN A CHAT ROOM?"

ESPECIALLY ONE THAT'S STILL UNDER CONSTRUCTION.

WITH NO WORKERS HERE ON THE WEEKEND, THERE'S NO ONE TO COME ACROSS THE MISSING GIRLS.

MMP!
RMPH!
JOE?!
I HEARD THAT--IT'S COMING FROM BEHIND THERE!

KAITLYN, RACHEL, OLIVA AND AUDREY!
THEY'RE ALL HERE!
PHEW!
BUT WHERE'S THE PERSON WHO BROUGHT THEM HERE?

SPA-LAOUSH!
AGAIN WITH THE AMBUSH FROM ABOVE?!
AND YOU ARE...?
MY NAME IS SARA.
BUT YOU CAN CALL ME...

CHAPTER EIGHT:
"THE SMARTEST GIRL IN THE WORLD"
ADMIT IT--NOT EVERYONE COULD HAVE FORMED THEIR OWN CIRCLE OF INTERNET FRIENDS...
...USING PEOPLE FROM REAL LIFE!
IT IS IMPRESSIVE, SARA.
CAN WE TALK ABOUT THIS AFTER WE'VE GOTTEN YOUR "FRIENDS" TO SAFETY?

NO!
KACK! KACK!
YOU'RE JUST JEALOUS! YOU'RE TRYING TO TAKE THEM AWAY FROM ME!
YOU JUST WANT ME TO BE LONELY!
BRILLIANT AND LONELY!
SHE MAY BE SMALLER THAN US--
--BUT SHE KNOWS HER KARATE.
THAT'S NOT GOING TO STOP ME FROM ENDING THIS BEFORE EVERYONE DROWNS!

WHAT ABOUT DROWNING IN DESPAIR?

YOU PROBABLY DON'T KNOW WHAT IT'S LIKE TO SIGN ONLINE...

... AND NEVER GET AN EMAIL.

NOT EVEN ONCE!

IT ALL SOUNDS VERY SAD.
NOW LET'S GO!
NO! MY FRIENDS AND I ARE HAVING FUN!
WE'RE NOT GOING ANYWHERE!
UAGH!
KRAK!
YOU CAN'T MAKE US!

SARA-- THEY'RE OBVIOUSLY HERE AGAINST THEIR WILL.
THERE ARE EASIER WAYS TO MAKE FRIENDS.
IT'S CLEAR YOU HAVE SOME...ISSUES.
WE'RE GOING TO MAKE SURE YOU GET THE HELP YOU NEED.
EH?!
KLAK!
YOU'RE JUST JEALOUS! BUT IF I CAN'T HAVE MY FRIENDS WITH ME...

...THEN NOBODY CAN!
SARA, DON'T DO ANYTHING STUPID.
SO FAR NO ONE HAS BEEN HURT. LET'S KEEP IT THAT WAY!

WHEN I FLIP THIS SWITCH, THE CURRENT RUNNING THROUGH THE TABLE SAW WILL BE COMPLETED!
SEE?! LISTEN TO ME:
I EVEN SOUND LIKE A SCIENCE GEEK.

HOWEVER YOU SAY IT, EVERYONE HERE IN THE WATER WILL BE ELECTROCUTED!
I KNOW YOU DON'T WANT THAT TO HAPPEN.

SURPRISE.
THAT'S EXACTLY WHAT I WANT!
SHUNKT!
N-NOTHING HAPPENED?!
I DON'T UNDERSTAND! WHERE'S THE ELECTRICITY RUNNING THROUGH THE SAW?!

SPLISH!

NO BIG MYSTERY, SARA.

I HAVE THE ANSWER RIGHT HERE!

ONCE I WAS UNDERWATER, I THOUGHT I COULD BE HELPFUL...

ALONG WITH THIS POWER CORD IN MY HAND.

UGHN?!

SEVERAL WEEKS LATER...
HALEY DANELLE AND HER FRIENDS ARE UNITED AGAIN..
... HAVING DECIDED TO SPEND A LITTLE LESS TIME ONLINE...
...AND MORE TIME LEARNING SOME REAL LIFE SKILLS.
CHAPTER NINE: "GTG! TTYL!"
OKAY, CLASS--THAT WAS AWESOME!

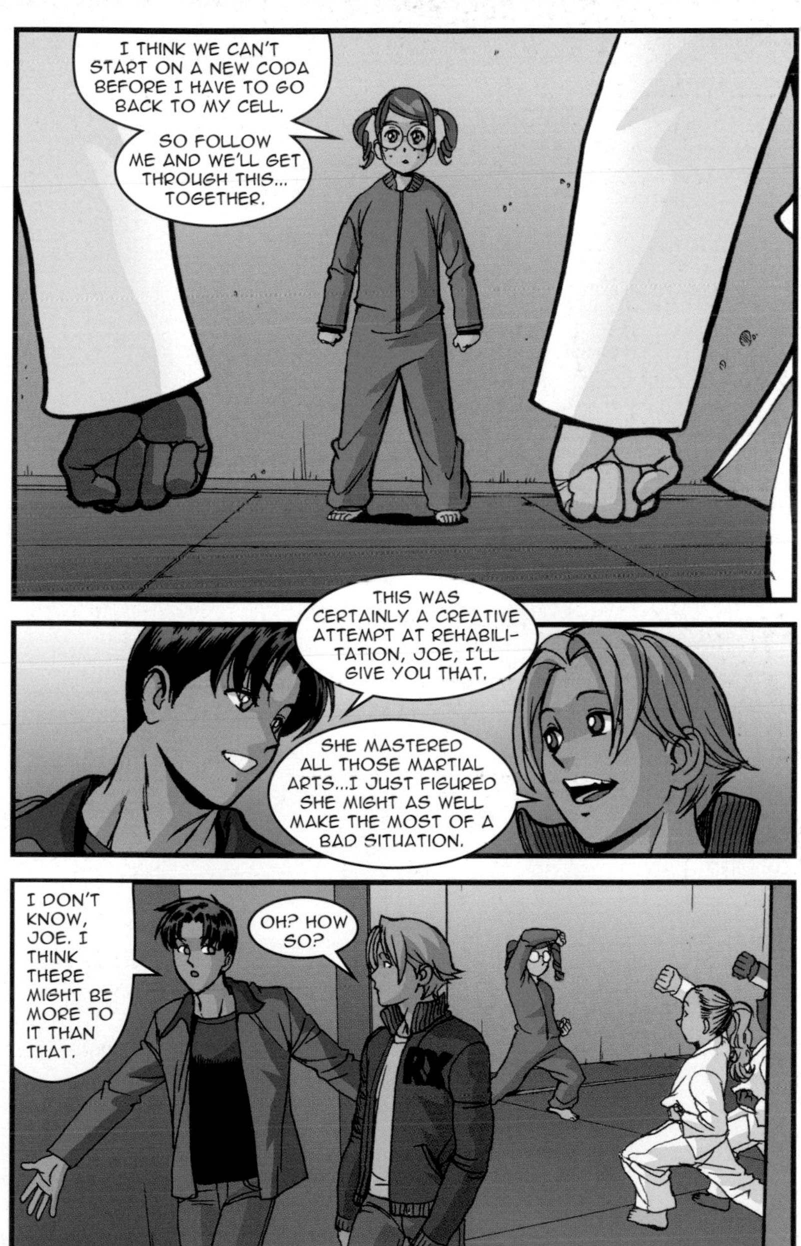
I THINK WE CAN'T START ON A NEW CODA BEFORE I HAVE TO GO BACK TO MY CELL.
SO FOLLOW ME AND WE'LL GET THROUGH THIS... TOGETHER.
THIS WAS CERTAINLY A CREATIVE ATTEMPT AT REHABILI-TATION, JOE, I'LL GIVE YOU THAT.
SHE MASTERED ALL THOSE MARTIAL ARTS...I JUST FIGURED SHE MIGHT AS WELL MAKE THE MOST OF A BAD SITUATION.
I DON'T KNOW, JOE. I THINK THERE MIGHT BE MORE TO IT THAN THAT.
OH? HOW SO?

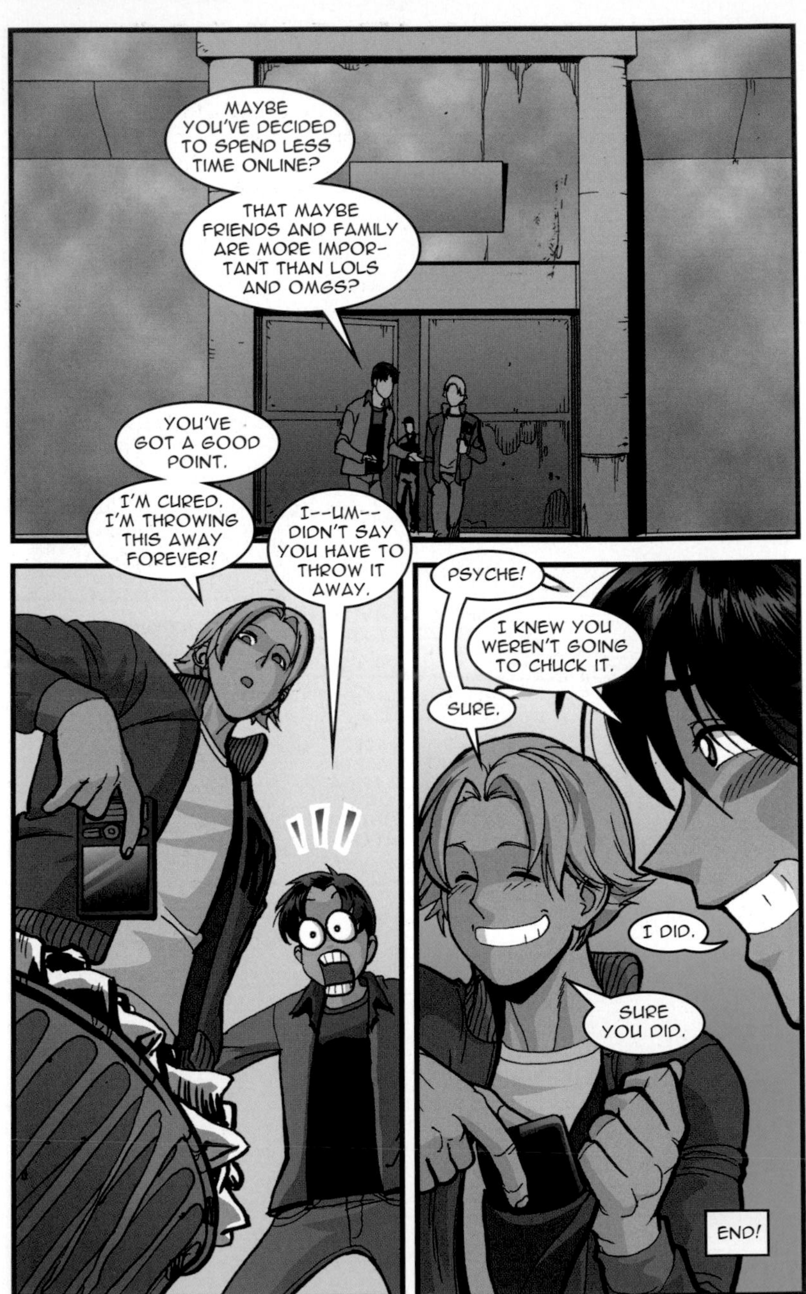

MAYBE YOU'VE DECIDED TO SPEND LESS TIME ONLINE?
THAT MAYBE FRIENDS AND FAMILY ARE MORE IMPOR-TANT THAN LOLS AND OMGS?
YOU'VE GOT A GOOD POINT.
I'M CURED. I'M THROWING THIS AWAY FOREVER!
I--UM--DIDN'T SAY YOU HAVE TO THROW IT AWAY.
PSYCHE!
I KNEW YOU WEREN'T GOING TO CHUCK IT.
SURE.
I DID.
SURE YOU DID.
END!

WATCH OUT FOR PAPERCUTZ™

Hi, mystery-lovers! Welcome to the second HARDY BOYS ADVENTURES graphic novel, filled with four stories featuring stage magicians, sagebrush, stuntwomen, and social media by Scott Lobdell, writer, and PH Marcondes and Tim Smith 3 artists, from Papercutz—those conscientious comic-makers dedicated to publishing great graphic novels for all ages. I'm Jim Salicrup, the Editor-in-Chief and honorary Undercover Brother.

"Piper Houdini" author Glenn Herdling, mesmerized by the magic in Tannen's Magic Store.

In "Abracadeath," Tim Smith 3 had to pull off a magic act of his own. Here for the very first time is the true story behind why the artwork by the very talented Mr. Smith 3 looks, shall we say, a bit rushed? Well, there's a good reason—it was. Not because Tim was in any way irresponsible, but because somehow he was given the wrong script to draw. So while doing a perfectly professional, polished job on a HARDY BOYS script, what Tim didn't know was that same script was already fully drawn by another artist (PH Marcondes) and soon to be published.

To be perfectly clear, it wasn't Tim's fault in any way, shape, or form that he was working on the wrong script. Sometimes mistakes happen, and this one was a doozy! By the time we all realized what had happed, the HARDY BOYS graphic novel that Tim should have been drawing—"Abracadeath"—was almost due. Tim, despite the overwhelming odds of completing 84 pages of comics in the remaining time left, agreed to do it... and as impossible as it seemed, he actually did it! Unfortunately, when an artist is working day and night, day after day with little sleep, the final result may not be his best work, but it's a miracle it exists at all. It's as if Tim pulled 84 pages of comic art out of a hat! What's impressive is not the work itself, but that he was able to do it at all. And for that we are all eternally thankful to Tim Smith 3.

Inside New York City's Tannen's Magic store.

The story in "Abracadeath" takes place in Bayport's answer to Hollywood's Magic Castle, a wonderful nightclub for magicians and magic enthusiasts, as well as the clubhouse for the Academy of Magical Arts. If you ever get the opportunity to see magic performed live, go for it! As fun as it is to watch magic performed on TV, say on *Penn & Teller: Fool Us*, it's far more amazing when you see it performed right before your eyes! I had a wonderful time there years ago with my friend Renee Witterstaetter. Closer to home, I recently had the good fortune to be invited by Glenn Herdling, the author of *"Piper Houdini,"* to attend a magic show at New York City's famed Tannen's Magic store. The store was mentioned in *"The Amazing Adventures of Kavalier & Clay"* the Pulitzer Prize winning novel by

Michael Chabon and I didn't realize that it was real and that it still existed. We got to see Noah Levine perform close-up magic and had a fantastic evening. And speaking of Glenn Herdling, you may want to check out *"Piper Houdini: Apprentice of Coney Island,"* a supernatural adventure about a young orphan in the 1920s who learns she is the niece of the legendary escape artist, Harry Houdini. Just go to http://piperhoudini.com/ for more information.

For our next trick, we want to present to you, not one, but two previews of Papercutz graphic novels we're sure you'll enjoy! Just simply go to the very next page and right before your eyes will appear an exciting sequence from THE ZODIAC LEGACY #2 "Power Lines," by Stan Lee, Stuart Moore, and PH Marcondes. If you enjoyed the runaway train in THE HARDY BOYS ADVENTURES #1, in "The Opposite Numbers," also drawn by PH Marcondes (and others), wait till you see what happens when Zodiac members Liam (The Ram), Roxanne (The Rooster), Duane (The Pig), and Malik (The Ox), without any help from the rest of their team, attempt to stop an even faster runaway train in France. (Can't get enough graphic novels with runaway trains? Then don't miss "The Disoriented Express" in NANCY DREW DIARIES #5. Papercutz aims to please.) Life may seem like a runaway train to twelve-year old Erik Farrell, THE ONLY LIVING BOY. He ran away from home and woke up as a "Prisoner of the Patchwork Planet." See how he tries to deal with it all in the preview written by David Gallaher and drawn by Steve Ellis.

Oops! We didn't mean to get so carried away talking about magic, but it's a subject that's close to our hearts. Somehow it's always seemed to be connected to comics in all sorts of surprising ways. From *Mandrake the Magician* to *Zatanna* to *Doctor Strange*, there have always been magicians of one sort or another in comics. So, before I run out of space (and they say space is infinite!), I better perform my final trick, and perform a vanishing act. Presto! I'm gone!

The cover of the first in a series of Piper Houdini books.

Thanks,

STAY IN TOUCH!

EMAIL:	salicrup@papercutz.com
WEB:	papercutz.com
TWITTER:	@papercutzgn
FACEBOOK:	PAPERCUTZGRAPHICNOVELS
FANMAIL:	Papercutz, 160 Broadway, Suite 700, East Wing, New York, NY 10038

Special Preview of THE ZODIAC LEGACY #2 "Power Lines" by Stan Lee, Stuart Moore, and PH Marcondes…

OKAY. YOU CAN DO THIS.

YOU CAN DO THIS.

YOU'RE A HERO.

UN, DEUX, TROIS…

EEEEEEEEEEEE

SPGGRKKKKK

ROX--
I HEARD! I STOPPED! I STOPPED ALREADY!
PULL ME BACK IN!
UHHHH--

WHUFF!

THAT WAS CLOSE.
GOOD THING NOTHIN' CAN HURT ME.
OH, GREAT!
NOTHING CAN HURT YOU!
WHAT ABOUT ME?

I, UH, DON'T WISH TO BE RUDE...
BUT WHAT ARE YOU GUYS DOING?

DUANE
The Pig
POWER: INFORMATION PROCESSING

WE'RE *TRYIN'* TO STOP THIS RUNAWAY TRAIN--
MAIS ILS N'Y RÉUSSISSENT PAS! *
NOTRE VITESSE EST MAINTENANT À 338 KILOMÈTRES À L'HEURE! **

*"BUT THEY ARE NOT SUCCEEDING!"

** "OUR SPEED IS NOW UP TO 210 MILES PER HOUR!"

YOU HAVING ANY BETTER LUCK?
THE FRENCH GOVERNMENT HAS SENT ME THEIR COMPUTER MODELS FOR THIS RAIL LINE...

Special Preview of THE ONLY LIVING BOY #1 "Prisoner of the Patchwork Planet" by David Gallaher and Steve Ellis
I DIDN'T DIE.

IN YA GO!
HERE'S THE THING, I DON'T CARE HOW RARE OR PRECIOUS YOU ARE.
I ONLY CARE ABOUT THE SCIENCE OF SECTAURIAN TRANS-SPECIES EVOLUTION. IT REALLY HAS ME WONDERING, PRINCESS...

...WHAT KIND OF CREATURE WILL YOU BECOME ?

THE KIND THAT DESTROYS YOU.

I DON'T THINK SO.
FETCH ME ANOTHER SUBJECT, ORDERLY.

ACTUALLY, JUST FETCH ME THAT ONE IN THE CAGE OVER THERE.

KLEEF?
DON'T WORRY... THEY AREN'T COMING FOR YOU.

I AM **KLEEF**. THIS IS **THE CENSUS**. THIS IS WHERE THE ABDUCTED AND THE ORPHANED COME TO DIE.

I CAME HERE WITH A FRIEND.

THERE ARE NO FRIENDS HERE, JUST PATIENTS. WE ARE LOCKED UP, PICKED APART, BRED TO FIGHT.

I DON'T WANT TO FIGHT.

NEITHER DID I.

BUT SOMETIMES, YOU HAVE TO FIGHT FOR WHAT YOU BELIEVE IN.

IS THERE A WAY OUT OF HERE? A WAY TO ESCAPE?
YEAH--THE ONLY WAY OUT IS TO LOSE. YOU WON'T FEEL SO LUCKY THEN. THEY'LL SEND YOU TO THE LAB, JUST LIKE THEY DID TO ME. IT MESSED ME UP.
THAT SOUNDS AWFUL.
IT AIN'T FUN. THEY TREAT YOU LIKE GARBAGE. AND BY THEY, I MEAN HIM...
DOCTOR ONCE.
MY DEAR, I WAS HOPING TO VIEW THE CHRYSALIS UNDER NATURAL CONDITIONS. BUT YOU CHOSE TO DEFY ME. WANT TO TRY IT AGAIN?
I'LL RIP YOU APART AND BREED AN ENTIRE FLYING ARMY FROM THE HUSK OF YOUR LIFELESS BODY.
AND THE GIRL? WHO IS SHE?
DANGEROUS.

IN YA GO!
HERE'S THE THING, I DON'T CARE HOW RARE OR PRECIOUS YOU ARE.
I ONLY CARE ABOUT THE SCIENCE OF SECTAURIAN TRANS-SPECIES EVOLUTION. IT REALLY HAS ME WONDERING, PRINCESS...
...WHAT KIND OF CREATURE WILL YOU BECOME?
THE KIND THAT DESTROYS YOU.
I DON'T THINK SO.
FETCH ME ANOTHER SUBJECT, ORDERLY.